Come Bye

White Wagon Books

Come Bye

Kathy Wagenknecht

Come Bye is a work of fiction. Names, places, and incidents are products of the author's imagination or are used fictitiously

Published by White Wagon Books

ISBN-13: 978-0615554181
ISBN-10: 0615554180

Cover painting: Pat White

Printed in the United States of America by CreateSpace

Dedication

For Judy and Cliff,
Joan and Wayne,
and all my other teachers and mentors.

With Special Thanks to Ann and Pam for early encouragement
and editing expertise.

One

"Never pay friends less than you would strangers unless they owe you money."

Velma Lee Lewis

She threw down her pen in disgust. The page before her was covered with splotches, blotches, and blots. She chuckled sourly thinking that **Splotches, Blotches and Blots** would be a better name for her going-nowhere book than **BellWhether Tails**. She tapped the top of the pen on her teeth. She had thought she had such a great idea. One so easy to do. One she could finish in a few weeks and generate some income, but she couldn't get any traction.

Gerry Krane knew she was in trouble. She told herself she just needed to generate income. But the truth was she needed cash. Fast. She'd thought she had a winner of an idea. She'd do a history of the renowned BellWhether Kennels through stories about their famous dogs. It was based on a project she'd started in high school. But after finding her old notebooks, surreptitiously interviewing Sally O'Neill and Belle Sheppard, spending days putting together an outline, and writing the first two chapters, she hated the whole idea. One chapter after another about all the dogs they'd owned didn't seem very appealing now. And it would take something damned appealing to get any funding from those two sharp business women.

Her dog, Jess, bumped her nose into Gerry's elbow, jamming the pen top into her gums. "Dammit, Jess! That hurt!" Gerry glared at Jess, then relented as the black and white bundle of energy looked up at her and whined.

"OK. Get your ball. I'll take you out for awhile. I know I haven't been much fun lately." Jess woo-wooed her approval and ran into the living room, nosed through the basket of toys, and scurried back down the slick hardwood floor with her ball in her mouth. Gerry smiled at Jess's antics. She really needed to find a job for Jess. She thought the dog must be bored silly doing little but watching Gerry write words and cross them out.

She opened the door to the deck and let Jess precede her out into the blazing July heat of Oklahoma. "Lord, Jess, I wish we could find you something to do that didn't involve being out in the heat."

"Find something for me, too."

Gerry, startled, jumped backward, landing on a squeaky toy that Jess had deposited there earlier. Its squawk further startled her as she jumped away and let fly a loud "Dammit!" She whipped around to find the cause of her jumping jacks, sending her chin-length red hair flying, and saw the grinning face of Winston Reynolds.

Nobody who knew him well called the gentle giant anything but Win, Smoke, or Marlboro Man – the latter two with heavy irony for this crusading ex-smoker now avid anti-smoking proselytizer.

"Smoke, you nearly scared me to death!" Gerry had sat down on the top step of the deck, catching her breath and throwing the ball for Jess.

Win bent his six-foot-eight frame to look into Gerry's green eyes. "You look okay to me." He straightened up and rummaged through his mail bag. "Got a letter for you. Looks official." He handed her a large envelope of a creamy, thick, bond paper addressed in beautifully lettered calligraphy.

She squeezed her brows together as she took the envelope. "Thanks, Smoke." She looked at the envelope carefully, front and back, and tried to read the smudged postmark. Still staring at the envelope, she shuffled to the door, called Jess, and went inside, forgetting to pull the door closed behind her.

"You're letting out all your cool," Win called before turning to walk away. "Though I think you lost most of it a long time ago," he muttered as he went.

Gerry pretended not to hear Win. She just didn't want to get into it with him. She tossed the envelope on her desk. "Come on, Jess," she called. "Let's get some water. We'll go back out later, after the sun goes down."

Bea removed her flowered bib apron and dropped it into the basket sitting at her feet. She tucked stray gray hairs into the bun at her nape, smoothed down the skirt of her print cotton dress, and opened the door of the diner. Another day of blazing heat, few customers, and aching feet. At least she could go home to her cool living room, prop her feet up in her recliner, and flip through the hundreds of channels on the satellite service until something mindless and mildly entertaining caught her interest. Later she would fall into bed for a night of tossing and turning, her legs aching so much they'd keep her awake. She felt like she was living a re-run, every day the same and all wearing her down.

Shep was waiting for her at the door to the screened porch. He wanted to play but had learned to wait until Bea had set down her purse, had dumped the dirty aprons and towels into the washer, and had fixed a glass of iced tea. Then he jumped against the door and whined until Bea got the Frisbee off the counter and opened the door.

A flip of her wrist sent the Frisbee flying and gave her time to get the mail and turn on the hose. She had perfected watering with her left hand while throwing the Frisbee with her right. It saved time and energy and she needed both in the unrelenting summer heat. But this time she stood staring at the large ivory envelope she had pulled out of the mail box, addressed to Josephine Murphy. Shep yipped at her to bring her back to the present. She shook her head, tucked the mail into her pocket, and turned on the hose.

Bea watered her legs and feet alternately with her flower beds. Shep began his "Jess's coming" dance. Gerry and Jess ambled across the yard toward Bea as Shep jumped and turned in circles.

"I see Jess's boyfriend is still happy to see her," called Gerry as she crossed into Bea's back garden.

Bea nodded and continued watering the hydrangeas. "How's your book coming?" she asked.

Shep and Jess circled the garden twice before Gerry responded with a sad shake of her head. "It's not. I don't think I can make it work. I've wasted so much time on it already that my financial situation is getting dire. You couldn't use any help at the diner, could you?"

Bea swung around in surprise, splashing Gerry's legs as she did. "Whoa!" Gerry yelled. "Actually, that felt great. Do it again." She stuck out a foot for Bea to water.

Bea complied. "I do need some help. But I can't pay much. Business is slow because of the heat. But I'd really like some time off. And I thought you couldn't cook."

Gerry frowned at Bea's babbling. "Yes, I can cook. I just don't like to cook for only myself." She took a breath. "Honestly, Bea, I really need some cash. Whatever you can pay me would be helpful."

"Let's try it out. Come in tomorrow. Cook breakfast. I'll pay minimum wage plus tips. See how it goes. Day by day. OK?"

"Thank you! It will give you a break while I look for something more permanent. What time tomorrow?"

"Six-thirty."

"See you then. Thank you! Thank you!" Gerry hurried back to her house. "Jess, come. We have to get ready for our new job!"

Bea gazed after her, frantically trying to decide if this was a good idea. She called to Shep, "Let's go veg out, boyo." He bounded up the steps ahead of her, wagging his tail into her legs as she opened the door. Bea walked through her house, closing drapes and blinds. Finally with all visual access blocked, she went into her bathroom, stripped off the cotton "housedress" she'd worn at the diner, and stepped into a cool shower. After pampering herself with expensive soap and shampoo, she dried with a fluffy towel and dressed in a pair of red silk pajamas. She wandered back into the kitchen where she mixed herself a stiff G & T before settling into her recliner.

Instead of flipping through endless channels of reality, news, sports, and game shows, she picked up the ivory envelope that had arrived today and studied the calligraphy. She absently patted the arm of her chair as she thought.

Shep pushed his head under her hand and flicked the tip of his tail back and forth. He wasn't sure what she wanted him to do. She wasn't sure either. Not about Shep nor herself. She'd turned herself into Andy Taylor's Aunt Bea to run the diner in the right persona. But maybe it was time to see if anybody else was still under her skin wanting out. Maybe that's why she was feeling so restless.

"Shep," she said to the best listener she knew, "do you think you'll like Josephine Murphy as much as you like Bea Murphy? Maybe I'll take a little trip and see if I still remember who I've been – JoJo, the tomboy; Josie, the high school girl; and Josephine, the potential sophisticate."

When Gerry got home that night she, too, bathed before sitting down at her desk. She eyed the envelope she still had not opened. She'd wait until tomorrow to open it. Maybe she could accumulate enough good karma to offset whatever loomed inside it.

And maybe her luck had turned. Bea hired her for the diner, she wouldn't starve working there, and she'd bought some time to come up with more money. But dammit, her best bet was still the book. She sighed heavily. She'd reread the two chapters she'd worked on earlier. Maybe she could salvage something.

BellWhether Tails

Thorpe – 1958

I had never heard such an edge of terror in Gran's voice before. "Sally, Gramps is hurt. Fell off his tractor. J.D.'s taking him to the hospital. Can you meet us there?"

I had a flash of my slightly stooped gray-haired grandfather lying in the wheat field while his green and yellow John Deere went down the row without him.

"Child, are you there?" Gran's voice slid up another notch on the fear scale.

I cleared my throat as I brushed aside the unwanted tear sliding down my cheek. "Yes, Gran, I'm here. And yes, I'll meet you at the hospital. I'll leave right away. See you shortly."

"Bless you," Gran murmured through a sigh as she disconnected.

For several moments I stared at my hands, my desk, the "wanted" posters on the bulletin board across from me, the bile-green walls, and finally focused on Margaret Pearson, the sixty-something glue that held together the fragile egos and dangerous duties of the Ford County, Kansas, Sheriff's Department.

"Mags," I started speaking before I reached her desk, "Gran just called. Gramps is hurt. I'm on my way to the hospital."

A flash of sympathy played across her face before she gave a curt nod. "Drop your call sheets on my desk before you leave. Anything hot?"

"No. Just a missing cat and a stolen car, but I don't think the cat can drive."

The left corner of Mags' mouth twitched. "Let us know how Will is. Go on, now." She pushed the air toward me as she spoke.

I didn't break any speed records getting to the hospital, but I knew I'd be there well before Gramps. The drive from their place took at least twenty minutes. I paced the halls, drank coffee, and worried until I saw J.D.'s rusty green Ford pickup pull up to the emergency entrance.

As I pulled open the door of the truck, I saw only Gran and J.D. inside the cab. J.D. flicked a thumb over his shoulder in answer to my puzzled look. Lying in the aptly named bed of the truck on a pallet of old quilts was Gramps, propped against bales of straw to keep him from shifting. Lines of pain creased his forehead above his tightly clenched eyes.

"Gramps?" I smoothed his hair and stroked his cheek. "Doing okay?"

"Mmm. Sal. Where are we?" His voice was a rough whisper.

"Hospital. Don't you know you're not supposed to jump off a moving tractor?" I attempted to bring a light touch to my question. I failed.

"Didn't. Knocked off." A spasm clenched his jaws and eyes even tighter.

A hand touched my arm. Gran's. Next to her was a wheelchair pushed by J.D.'s grandson, Jimmy. Gran turned to him, "I don't think he can sit. Can you get a stretcher?"

Jimmy popped a wheelie and took off at a lope. Within minutes, he and a nurse were guiding a gurney across the sidewalk. Gran stayed next to Gramps, laying a soft hand on his arm to reassure and calm him. Jimmy and the efficiently compact nurse gently loaded Gramps onto the gurney and wheeled him into the hospital.

After we sent J.D. home with our hearty thanks, Gran and I found seats in the Emergency Waiting Room. "What happened, exactly? Did you see it?" I asked her gently.

Gran's eyes were fixed on the door into the examination area, willing it to open to someone bringing news. Without changing her focus, she said flatly, "I didn't see it. I just heard Thorpe barking like crazy from his pen. When I went out to see what was wrong, I saw the tractor run into a tree, then keep spinning its wheels, going nowhere." She glanced at me then turned back to the door.

"Where was Gramps?"

"I couldn't see him. I was afraid he'd had a stroke and lost control of the tractor. I let Thorpe out, and he tore off up the hill, barking constantly until he stopped a couple hundred feet behind the tractor. He stood there barking until I got there. Will was crumpled on the ground, moaning, and trying to get up. I left Thorpe with him, ran back to the house to call J.D.'s place for help, then went back to Will. J.D. came with his truck, and we loaded him into it. I called you, and we got here as quick as we could." She leaned back, sighing, before patting me on the arm. "Thanks for coming." She turned back to the door, crossed her arms across her chest, squared her feet in front of her chair, and sat up straight.

I stood and walked to the admission desk. I hadn't been a deputy long, only a couple of months, but I knew that my uniform could sometimes bring faster results. "Any news on Will O'Neill? I'm his granddaughter." My official, polite voice got the attention of the clerk who looked up from her paperwork. She asked me to wait a moment, and placed a call from the red phone sitting on her desk.

After a cryptic conversation whose only words I understood were "Will" and "O'Neill", she replaced the receiver and looked up at me. "He's being taken for x-rays. They're checking for broken bones and internal injuries. The doctor will be able to tell you something in about an hour. Why don't you go have a cup of coffee while you wait?" She pointed down the hallway beside her to the entrance to the cafeteria.

I cajoled Gran into going with me for a bite to eat. She understood the logic. In fact, she's the one who had taught it to me. If you're worried, eat. If you're scared, eat. If you want to comfort someone, feed her. Coffee and a piece of surprisingly good chocolate pie helped both of us to bat down the knot of fear lurking in our gullets.

After what seemed like several days but was actually about an hour and a half, the doctor found us. "Mrs. O'Neill, I am Dr. Dennis Jones. I just finished examining your husband and admitting him to the hospital. He has a broken pelvis and will have to be kept immobile for quite some time. I don't want to say how long, yet. We'll see how he progresses. They're taking him up to a room right now. Wait about fifteen minutes, then you can go see him. Room 202."

"Doctor, is the broken pelvis his only injury?" I was still worried about the possibility of internal bleeding.

"That and being generally banged up from the spill he took. He'll heal. It will be painful and slower than he'd like, but he'll heal. He told me he's a tough old bird." He slightly smiled at Gran.

"That he is." Gran pursed her lips. "Are you telling us everything, young man?"

"Yes, ma'm. Everything I know right now. I've given him something to help with the pain. He'll probably sleep. After you've checked on him, why don't you two go home and get some rest and come back tomorrow? We'll have more information about how he's doing by then."

Gran nodded, and I answered him, "Thanks, Dr. Jones. We'll see you tomorrow."

We peeked in on Gramps then headed for the ranch. As soon as we got there, Gran insisted on checking on Thorpe. "He was so upset when I penned him. Go let him out, Sal, would you?"

I found him sitting at the door to his run. He looked at me, cocked his head, and whined. I opened the gate for him, expecting him to dash out. Instead, he walked to me and bumped his head into my left hand that hung at my side. I rubbed the top of his head as he leaned against my leg. Then he moved slowly away, looking back over his shoulder at me as he did. He stopped at the edge of the field where the sun's last rays tinged his black and white fur with a backlit fiery halo.

He dropped into the classic border collie crouch, front end lower than back end, and looked intently at me. Gramps called it "the eye," that intense watching that border collies do instinctively. He looked from me to the field and back at me. He waited. He looked at the field again, then back to me. He wanted something.

"Thorpe, I don't know what you want," I said softly.

He whined and looked quickly at the field before directing his disconcerting gaze back at me.

"Do you want to go to the field?" I pointed in the direction he'd been looking.

He took a few steps before stopping to watch me. I pointed. He whined as he took a few steps. He looked back at me again.

Exasperated at my ignorance, I threw out my hand to point at the field and said loudly, "Go!"

He went. Running at full speed toward the horizon, he soon disappeared from my sight. I stood stock still, feeling vulnerable to Thorpe's demands. Then I saw the first of the cattle come into view as they were directed into the pasture just west of the house. Before I could believe it possible, Thorpe had moved about thirty cows and calves into the large fenced area and barked at me from the gate.

I closed it. I told him what a wonderful dog he was as he went back to his run, threw his food bowl into the air, and barked.

"Got it." I fed him, closed the gate to his run and walked up to the house.

"I just got my first herding lesson," I told Gran. She smiled and asked if I was ready to eat.

The next day at the hospital, I entertained Gramps with the story of my previous night's exploits. His doctor had told us to limit our visit to an hour so that Gramps could get plenty of rest. He needed to sleep to heal, the doctor declared, but I thought laughter was an even better solution. I embellished my tale until both Gramps and Gran were chortling.

"Gramps, where did you get Thorpe? And why did you name him that?"

"Long story, Sal. Got him in Lawrence, at the Haskell Indian Institute. He was already named. Ask your Gran." He smiled at both of us and closed his eyes.

I peppered Gran with questions as I went first to the Sheriff's office to clear some additional time off then to my house to pick up some clothes.

"OK, hush, child. I'll tell you if you quit interrogating me." She patted my hand to take the sting out of the words. I'd been accused of being too eager a questioner before. My father used to call me "The Grand Inquisitor."

Gran started her story as I turned out of town. "About four years ago while you were living up in Topeka, J.D. asked Will to drive up to Lawrence with him. It was right after his mother died, and he needed to deliver some of the family furniture to his sister. Her husband teaches at KU. J.D. wanted some company for the drive. He said they could spend a night with his sister, see a little of the town, and be home by the following evening.

"Will and I discussed it, and I urged him to go. He so rarely gets off the farm.

"So they went. When they got back, J.D. had a dog, Thorpe, with him. He'd got him from some Navajo kid at

Haskell Institute. You know, the Indian school. The kid had an emergency and needed money. He sold his dog to J.D."

"J.D. was proud of getting that dog. Told everyone how it was named after Jim Thorpe, the decathlon gold medalist who had gone to Haskell. Talked about how the dog could herd sheep and cattle and was going to make his life so much easier."

We had arrived home by then. Gran kept talking as she walked to the house. "About a month later, J.D. came over to talk to Will. Had Thorpe with him. Acted like it was some important private matter. I left them alone. Pretty soon, Will came in with the dog. Said he was going to buy it from J.D.

"I just stared at him. I knew he'd tell me when he got ready.

"He shuffled his feet, ruffled Thorpe's hair and left. The next morning he took the dog to the field with him. He talked to Thorpe, watched him with the cattle. He'd talk and throw his arms around. After about a week, he told me to come out with them.

"He said something I didn't quite catch to Thorpe and threw an arm up then out. Thorpe took off through the fields and before long was back with the cattle. Will was busting at the seams with pride. He praised Thorpe to high heavens, fed him something he got out of his pocket, and stood there grinning. From then on, Will and Thorpe were inseparable, a team. Will trusted Thorpe to do his job, and Thorpe trusted Will."

I had been biting my tongue to keep from interrupting Gran during the telling. But now that she'd paused, I thought I could throw out a few questions. "So why did J.D. sell Thorpe to Gramps?"

Gran smiled, "He couldn't get the dog to do anything." She kept smiling as she pulled food from the refrigerator and set it on the table. Dinner with Gran always consisted of about twenty dishes — at least one meat, five vegetables, bread, pickles, and dessert. I set the big old oak table with only two places. I caught Gran looking at Gramps' empty spot as she set the last of the pickles on the table.

After my parents were killed in a car crash while I was living in Topeka, my home base was this ranch. This room.

This table. Fresh pangs of grief hit me as I thought about the missing places at the table. I pulled myself together, served myself, caught my breath, and asked another question. "So how did Gramps get Thorpe to herd?"

Gran chuckled, "He called Haskell Institute and got ahold of the kid who'd trained Thorpe. Name of Windrunner. Will offered to give him back, but the kid said it was a fair deal. Then the kid taught him a few words of Navajo and told him the arm motions to use."

I frowned as I asked, "Why didn't J.D. ask the kid when he got Thorpe?"

"Stubborn. Thinks he's such a good dog trainer. Wouldn't ask for help."

"Then why'd he sell the dog? Seems like that would make him look like a failure."

"You don't know J.D. very well. Nothing's ever his fault. He told Will that he'd noticed how much Will liked the dog when they were driving back from Lawrence. And he'd decided it wasn't fair to the dog not to use him to herd since he was going to be riding his new horse to round up his cattle."

"You don't like J.D. much, do you?"

Gran didn't say anything, just gave me her famous sidelong glance.

"Gramps surely didn't believe the horse story. Why'd he buy Thorpe?"

"Will had really been taken with the dog. He was glad to get him. Especially when they'd taught each other how to work together. And J.D. is angry. Has said he got the short end of the stick. Stubborn old fool."

When we went to see Gramps the next day, I had another story to tell him about Thorpe. "Last night after dinner I went out to check on the animals. Thorpe was sitting at the gate to his kennel and yipped when he saw me. I opened the gate to let him out, but he didn't move. He yipped again so I went into the kennel to see what was wrong. Huddled into the corner behind him was a mewing lump, a tiny black kitten hidden in the shadows. I picked it up, told Thorpe what a good boy he was, and carried the kitten back to the house. Gran said she thought we should keep it. The mice were starting to overrun the barn since the old tom died. I named him Shadow."

Gramps nodded, "Good name. You liking Thorpe?"

"He's amazing. I can't believe that J.D. just let him go."

Gramps looked over the top of his glasses at me, "Hon, J.D. might be neighborly, but nobody ever accused him of being smart."

Gran's lip twitched in the corner as she patted Gramps' arm. "Thorpe's almost got Sally trained. I 'spect they'll be a good team before long."

Gramps nodded again. "Good. He needs to work. He can't just be ignored while I'm laid up. Take care of him, Sal, and he'll take care of you."

I patted his other arm.

After Gramps came home from the hospital, I went back to work at the Sheriff's office, but moved some clothes out to the ranch so I could stay there most nights. It was just easier — working until dark then falling into bed rather than having to drive the twenty-five minutes back to town each night. Of course, I drove in every morning, but I wasn't so tired then.

Luckily, not much beyond routine was happening at work. It wasn't full summer yet so the heat-related crime hadn't started. There were as always a few drunks, a few fights, a few thefts, and a few missing animals to deal with, but these I could handle with my mind engaged on what I needed to do at the farm.

Thorpe and I got into the habit of working with the cattle every morning before I went to work and every evening after I got home. He was alert, funny, and good company. I don't think I could have handled all the work I did that summer if I hadn't had Thorpe at my side. I always stopped to tell Gramps about Thorpe after each of our work sessions. It made a rhythm to the days.

Finally, Gramps was well enough to get back to work. "Sally, I'll never be able to thank you enough for stepping up and taking care of this place while I've been down." Gramps' ears were red with embarrassment as he talked seriously to me. "And thank you for taking care of Thorpe. He means a lot to me."

"Oh, Gramps, he's come to mean a lot to me, too. He's fun to work with. You know, I heard from one of the guys at work that there are herding contests — trials, he called them. You can enter with your dog and try to do the best job of gathering up the cattle in the shortest time. I think Thorpe would be great at that."

"Why don't you enter with him? I bet you could win."

"You wouldn't mind? I think it would be a lot of fun."

"I know a guy who does that. Jim Williams. I'll introduce you to him. Bet he could tell you all about it."

Within a week, I was signed on as a student and unpaid apprentice to Jim Williams. If I'd help him feed his animals every evening, he'd teach me the rules of herding trials.

Miss Kitty – 1960

I felt eyes on my back. I turned quickly to see who was watching me but saw only a flash of white turn the corner. I took a few steps toward the corner then stopped. I wasn't sure I wanted to know.

I went instead through the double glass doors of the Ford County Administrative Offices, turned right down the hallway and into the Sheriff's Department. "Mags," I nodded at my boss as I hung up my coat and sat down at my gray steel desk. I opened the bottom drawer, careful to keep my nyloned legs away from its rough edges, and tucked my purse inside. I willed my heart to still.

"You okay, Edie?" Mags glanced at me over the top of her half-moon reading glasses, "You look pale."

"Feel pale." I pulled out several folders and placed them on my desk. Just lined up pencils, pens, and a ruler in front of me.

"Sick? There's a bug going around," she proclaimed while writing onto the large blotter in front of her. Her gray curls bobbed as she turned her head from side to side as she read from the stack of papers on her left and transcribed it onto the blotter.

"No. Just pale." I didn't want to talk about it. Didn't want to think about it. Didn't want to admit how afraid I was that someone was watching me. I'd come to Dodge City to escape. I hoped I wouldn't have to get out of Dodge this soon. I'd only begun to feel comfortable here: know the details of my job as a clerk, rent a comfortable little house, buy a car, meet a few people. I stared at the back of Mags' head as I remembered my days of running, hitchhiking, working odd jobs, looking over my shoulder, hiding.

A hand waved in front of my eyes. "Hello? Bell? Anybody home?" Sally O'Neill always called me Bell. Refused to call me Edie. Said it sounded like a lounge singer.

"Sorry, Sally. Need something?" I looked into her smiling eyes and had the bad luck to blush.

"What's wrong, Bell?" The warm concern in her voice nearly undid me. I almost told her.

"Nothing. You just startled me." I didn't look at her but shuffled through the papers in one of the folders I'd laid on the desk.

She watched me a few more seconds then shrugged and went to her desk. She flipped through the top layer of papers, and pulled one out. She studied it before tucking it into her notebook and turning to leave. I kept my eyes on her reflection in the glass of the framed picture of the governor hanging across from my desk. She paused again as she neared my desk, took a breath, opened her mouth, closed it, and walked hurriedly past me on her way to the door.

Close call.

I stayed at the office late that evening. I wanted everyone to be gone before I left. I didn't want an audience for whatever awaited me. After straightening my desk twice, I forced myself to go. I nearly goose-stepped down the hallway holding my head high and back straight. I was getting prepared.

Once outside I scanned up and down. Nothing. Nobody loitering. Nobody watching. Nothing.

I let out the breath I didn't know I was holding. I took three steps toward my car before I felt the eyes again. I whirled around and saw — nothing. Heart pounding, I made it to my car, threw open the door and slid in as I pulled the door closed behind me. I sat very still. I patted the dash of my newly purchased car, thanking God that I wasn't on foot.

It had been a while since I had a car. I'd forgotten how safe and how free it felt. And I liked this car even though it was ten years old. It was turquoise and white, well-kept, and clean. It suited me.

As my heart rate slowed and the nausea subsided, I found my keys and stabbed the right one into the ignition. I put my foot on the clutch and turned my head, ready to back away from the curve. Something stopped me. A sound, like a whine or cry. I let out the clutch and depressed it again. No. No squeak. I looked around using the mirrors and still saw nothing.

Figuring I could sit there and scare myself to death or drive home, I chose the second option and slowly crept the six blocks to my house, skipping the planned trip to the grocery store. I could eat eggs. It didn't matter. I wasn't hungry. I parked in front of the small house that was mine for at least the next year and carefully looked around. I saw nobody, but felt like I was being watched again.

Shrugging in resignation, I got out of my car and walked up the path to the door. As I passed a large arborvitae tree, I thought I saw movement. I turned to the tree with my hands on my hips. "Dammit! I am tired of this. If you want something, come and get it!"

Nothing.

Disgusted with myself, I turned away just as I heard the whine again. I wheeled back around shouting, "Now, dammit! Come here and quit playing with me."

I saw movement under the bottom branches of the tree. I bent down to look and heard the whine. Then I saw white furry legs followed by the rest of a middle-sized black and white dog belly-crawl out from under the tree. The dog stood and looked at me. Its head was low and its butt high. It stared straight into my face, its eyes unmoving.

"Oh, no! Not an attack dog on top of everything else. Well, hell with it!" I moved slowly past the dog toward my house. I climbed onto the porch, opened the door, and went inside. The dog didn't take its eyes off me. It didn't move at all.

The next morning, the dog still hadn't moved. Same place; same stance. "Have you been here all night?" I asked it while slowly making my way to the car.

I pulled away from the curb and saw the dog move behind me. As I rolled down the street, it moved into an easy lope, following me. I arrived, parked, and started walking toward my building while the dog watched. When I was about ten steps away from the car, it curled up in the shade under the car and watched me walk into the building.

Mags was on the phone as I passed her desk on the way to mine. After she hung up, she looked over at me in concern. "You don't look any better today than yesterday. Shouldn't you be home in bed?"

I shook my head. "No. I'm okay." I messed with folders and papers for a few minutes before asking, "Mags, you know anything about dogs?"

Mags shook her gray curls, "No. Got cats. Ask Sal."

"Ask Sal what?" Sally asked as she swung past my desk, cup of coffee in one hand, donut in the other.

I felt the blood rise in my cheeks. "Dogs," I mumbled. "You know anything about dogs?"

Sally looked puzzled, but nodded, "Some. I do some herding. Why?" Her gaze didn't waver. Reminded me of the dog.

I finally cleared my throat and said, "A dog's been following me."

"When you were walking?"

"No. In my car."

"A dog's following you in your car? Barking?"

I shook my head, "Mmm. Doesn't bark. Just follows me. Then lays under the car when I park."

"How far does it follow you?"

"From home. About a mile."

"Just today?"

"No. I think it followed me home yesterday."

Sal grinned, "You dragging a pork chop?"

I rolled my eyes. "It's weird. The dog stands with its head down and butt in the air and stares at me. Gives me the creeps."

A smile spread across Sally's freckled face. "Black and white dog, about two feet tall and three feet long?"

"Yeah. You know the dog?"

"No, but I think it's a border collie." She turned to Mags, "Anybody report a lost border collie or sheep dog?"

Mags shook her head without looking up, "Don't think so."

Sally looked out the window then back at me. "Come on, Bell. Let's go check on your dog."

"It's not my dog," I muttered as I followed her out.

When we neared the car, the dog looked up and whined. Sally squatted down a few feet from it and spoke softly to it, "Come here baby. Come to Sally. That's a good baby, come on." As she spoke the dog slowly crawled from under the car and stood up in the same weird stance. Sally crooned and cooed, "Good dog. Good baby." She stood and took a tentative step toward the dog. It spread its front legs and dropped its head lower. Sally took another step, holding a hand, palm up, toward the dog. She repeated, "Good dog, good baby," as she waited.

The dog raised its head and sniffed her hand. Sally reached down and patted its chest. Reassured it with her words and gentle touch. After a few minutes, she patted the dog's neck and flank. She said softly, "It's wearing a collar." She eased nearer and felt around the collar, locating a tag caught in the dog's coat.

"Dog's name is Kitty." She smoothed the fur around its neck, "Hey, Kitty, girl. It's okay."

"For God's sake! Kitty!" I blurted. The dog turned to me, her tail wagging slightly.

Sally looked up at me from her kneeling position in front of the dog, "She likes you."

"She's been stalking me!"

Sally studied the tag attached to Kitty's collar. "Remember this address: 1214 Elm." She straightened up and said something soft to Kitty, who lay back down under the car. Sally headed back to the office and said, "Let's go check out 1214 Elm."

Within a few minutes, Sally was sitting at her desk surrounded by binders, ledgers, file folders, and loose sheets of paper. In a few more minutes, she let out a whoop. "It's the car! It's the damned car!"

"What's the car?" Mags glared at Sally as she put her first finger over her pursed lips in the universal librarian signal for "Shhh."

I said quietly, "The dog's following the car? Not me?"

Sally's eyes twinkled with mischief. She bundled up all her research materials and dropped them on my desk. "Figure it out." She swung toward the hallway and whistled something from a cartoon's soundtrack as she nearly skipped out the door.

I stared at all the files, binders, and loose pages on my desk. Did I even care enough to try to find out? Of course.

It took me nearly an hour to retrace Sally's trail. She was more familiar with the documents and sources. And she was a detective.

When she came back to the office I was waiting. I'd made notes. She leaned over my desk with raised eyebrows. I responded, "1214 Elm was owned by Bertha Morrow, who died last month. She also owned a 1950 turquoise and white Chevy that her niece sold to Baker Motors. Where I bought it."

Sally nodded. I continued, "Kitty disappeared after Bertha died. Nobody's seen her since. According to the neighbor, Bertha loved Gunsmoke. Named the dog after Amanda Blake's character."

Sally's smile lit her eyes. "You did good. Now what?"

"Now what what?"

"What are you going to do with Miss Kitty?"

I shook my head, "Nothing."

"You're just going to let her herd your car from now on?"

"Oh. Well. Hmm."

"I think she picked you."

"I think she found the car."

"OK, then. Call the pound. They'll pick her up."

I felt my eyes widen, "And do what with her?" Sally lifted her eyebrows. I felt a warning tug. I hadn't let anything get close for three years. "OK," I sighed. "What do I need to buy?"

Sally winked as she pulled a piece of paper from her pocket and handed it to me.

I read, "Food, toys, bed, leash. Dr. McAdams – vet." I stared at the list, resigned. I guess I had a dog.

Maybe they would do, Gerry mused. She wasn't even sure what she thought was wrong with them earlier. She flipped through the pages twice more before deciding she'd write another "tail" or two before she completely gave up on her project.

The four houses on a dusty track that intersected the back road to Edith on the west and the long driveway to BellWhether Kennels on the east had a mailing address of Plainview, Oklahoma, but there really was no town of Plainview any more. It had died and blown into Kansas on the steady winds that never stopped on their long trip from Texas.

Besides Bea's and Gerry's houses, two more houses survived on the Road to Nowhere, as Gerry called the dusty trail. One belonged to Win Reynolds since his mother died – the shady oasis surrounded by trees watered by three generations of Reynolds gardeners.

The other had belonged to old Mr. Clark until he died last fall. His estate had been tied up while his lawyer tried to locate his heirs, but was finally settled and the house put up for sale. It just recently sold to an artist from Arkansas. She hadn't moved in yet, and nobody knew anything about her except that she supposedly had a young son, and that she was moving to Plainview to get away from the distractions of her previous life.

Speculation about the artist had been the main topic of conversation among the customers of the Edith Diner for the last several weeks. Bea was tired of it and had refused to play along. But Gerry was fresh meat, perfect for more guesswork and gossip.

"Hey, Gerry. You working here now?" A tall gray haired rancher in a faded blue shirt and jeans greeted her as he took his place at a table filled with other gray-haired or balding ranchers.

"Yep. For a little while. Giving Bea a break. What can I get you, Red?" She wondered about the "Red" since his gray hair and tanned-leather face had nothing about them to suggest "Red." Maybe his hair had been red when he was younger. She could still see a few freckles along the tan line of his arms and a few remnants of pale pink skin underneath his ice-blue eyes.

"Cuppa coffee and sweet roll, sugar." Red winked at Gerry. "Hey, don't you live next door to Bea?"

Gerry nodded as she poured Red's coffee.

"So what do you know about your new neighbor? I hear she's a big-time artist."

Just as Gerry started to respond, she caught Bea's eye and the slight shake of her head. Gerry looked back to Red, "Hmm. I hadn't heard."

Red snorted in disgust. He was hoping for fresh gossip grist.

Gerry went into the kitchen to fry two eggs for another inquisitive rancher. "These guys are worse than a bunch of sorority girls. Is gossip all they do?"

Bea cocked her head and raised an eyebrow. "Were you a sorority girl?"

"Damn! Me and my mouth! Please don't tell. I'd never hear the end of it." Gerry clasped her hands under her chin and cast up pleading eyes to Bea.

Bea snorted, "Your secret's safe with me. Better watch those eggs."

By mid-morning, Gerry was getting a strong flavor of how hard Bea worked at the diner. She let her tired mind wander as she cooked. She'd grown up in Edith, knew most of the old ranchers as friends of her father or grandfather. Then she left and went to Fayetteville to school at the University of Arkansas. Whoo! Pigs! Sooie!

There she'd pledged Alpha Kappa Alpha, made good grades, got a degree with honors in English lit and left to find a way to put her degree to work. She worked in Tulsa for a couple of years as an administrative assistant to an insurance exec. Made pretty good money. She saved all she could and moved back home, buying an old house in Plainview and planning to write a book.

Now she'd run out of money and ideas and had ended up frying eggs in the diner. What a success she'd made!

Bea watched emotions flicker across Gerry's mobile face. She thought she knew what Gerry must be feeling, winding up with a crap job in her hometown after escaping to college and its promise of a different life.

"Gerry, those eggs are probably ready."

Gerry started, then looked down at the skillet. "Thanks, Bea. They're perfect. I guess you get better at timing with practice."

"And watching," Bea winked.

Gerry blushed, "I was daydreaming. Sorry."

Gerry plated the eggs as Bea opened the large refrigerator. "What do you want to cook for lunch and dinner? All we need is some sort of sandwich and a blue-plate special. There's plenty of food. I've got hamburger, chicken, pork chops, pork loin, and bacon. For veggies, there are potatoes, sweet potatoes, cabbage, zucchini, tomatoes, onions, and bell peppers. Then there's peaches and blackberries. And they won't last another day."

"Hmm. Well, blackberry cobbler seems obvious. And tomato, peach and onion relish. Maybe coleslaw, roasted white and sweet potatoes in French fry cuts, and roast pork loin. All of the above for the blue plate and chicken with the potatoes and slaw for the sandwich plate. Do you think grilled or salad for the chicken?"

"Since it's so beastly hot, maybe a chicken salad. And you could stuff a tomato with it rather than put it on a sandwich."

"That sounds great. How many do I cook for?" Gerry carried the assembled breakfast to the doorway.

Bea smiled and shook her head. "That's the hard part. Serve the meal and then we'll talk."

Gerry was back before Bea had finished writing the menu on the blackboard. "Don't forget to post the menu on the board early in the day. Lots of folks stick their heads in to see what's on before deciding whether to eat here later."

Gerry nodded and made a note on the pad she took from her apron pocket.

"Also, I try to think of something else I can use the cooked food for if I have a lot left over. For example, I don't make up all the boiled chicken into salad. I'll hold off until I need it. Then if I don't use it all, it can go in the freezer, in a soup, in a casserole, etc."

Gerry nodded as she wrote, "I see. So the pork loin can be the sandwich tomorrow?"

"You got it." Bea looked pleased.

Gerry felt the blood in her cheeks again. She hated her propensity for blushing but hadn't figured out yet how to stop it. She pretended that the heat in the kitchen rather than praise colored her cheeks.

Two

"Never pretend to be who you haven't been."
Velma Lee Lewis

Belle, one of the unknowing subjects of Gerry's book, wiped the sweat from her face and neck with the bandana in her pocket. Since it had gotten so beastly hot, she had been rising very early to work the dogs in the relative cool of the morning. But it was ten o'clock now, and her outdoor hours were over until evening.

She fixed herself a large glass of iced lemonade and sat in her worn leather chair at her oversized oak desk in the kennel office. It contained a small fan in one corner and a stack of pink slips under a horseshoe in the opposite one. She loved the clean expanse of the mellow wood that was her desktop. She turned on the small oscillating fan so that it moved the conditioned air past her in cooling waves. Her left hand pushed her hair up and to the left off her face. Cool air dried it quickly. As she sipped her cold drink, she looked with satisfaction at the phone messages: six inquiries for trained dogs.

She had three promising young dogs she was starting in herding. She intended to place them as trained working dogs, commanding very high prices. She believed her customers got their money's worth – she spent many hours making the dogs look brilliant and immediately valuable to their new owners.

She often wished that she could do more training of the owners so that they would train their own dogs even though she actually preferred working with dogs than with most people. But everyone wanted instant results, so she created "instant herders."

Of course Sally had the same problem with her big sniffers. Bloodhounds could track, as border collies could herd, but they needed training and direction. Sally was successful in requiring her customers to attend training classes before they could take their dogs home. But her customers were primarily from law enforcement organizations who follow rules better than ranchers do.

Belle's steel gray hair was cut short to allow her to ignore it most of the time. She kept it clean and brushed it in the morning, most days, but after that her fingers shoved it off a hot forehead many times a day. It was such a habit that the kennel staff used it to indicate in silence when the boss was coming.

Sally O'Neill, the other boss, had her tapping cane to alert the staff as it alerted Belle to stop daydreaming.

"Done with the pups already?" Sally asked as she entered the kennel office. Her desk was a large table stacked high with big books, files, and unusual items like muffin tins and sledge hammers. It was made of a lovely pumpkin pine, but it had been years since anyone had seen its warmly glowing top. Sally wanted everything in view. She had no use for drawers.

She pushed a few catalogs aside and set down her coffee cup – her orange coffee cup that nobody else had better try to use. That orange cup was her constant companion from the time she crawled out of bed in the morning until she fell into it again at night.

Belle nodded to Sally, "I'm done. Done in. This heat! How can you drink coffee?"

Sally ignored the dig. It was a longstanding squabbling point. Sally swore that coffee didn't make her hot. Belle insisted that it did – the hot liquid warmed the body and the caffeine caused hot flashes. They argued their positions good-naturedly and frequently.

"I've got a training class next week. Ten folks coming back for their ten-thousand-mile checkup. Four are women. Times sure have changed. Used to go years between women handlers.

Anyway, I hope it cools off before then or we'll have to do all our field exercises at night." She adjusted the thick braid of hair at the back of her head. Down, her hair nearly reached her waist, but she'd worn it in a braid for more years than she cared to count.

Belle watched Sally adjust the hairpins and said archly, "Be cooler without that hair, too."

Sally looked over the top of her glasses, her brown eyes snapping. "And you'd be shorter without your feet," she said softly.

Belle's gray eyes sparkled as she thought up a reply, but she noticed that Sally wasn't paying attention to their ongoing verbal fencing. Instead, she was holding a large ivory envelope, rubbing her hand over it, even smelling it. Her eyes were unfocused as she lay it down in front of her and lightly smoothed it with two fingers.

"Sally, you OK?" Belle looked with concern at her friend of nearly fifty years.

Sally nodded. She picked a second envelope from the stack of mail and held it toward Belle. "One here for you, too."

Belle frowned as she got up and took three steps before she could reach the envelope Sally held toward her. She moved back to her chair, sat, and held the thick bond envelope up to the light. What was it that felt so unsettling about that envelope, addressed to Belle Sheppard at BellWhether Kennels? The lettering was beautiful, the texture of the paper rich and creamy. She stared at it without opening it for several seconds.

A knock on the door interrupted her stupor. She laid the envelope down with a sigh of relief and said loudly, "Come in."

It was two o'clock in the afternoon before Sally again looked at the ivory envelope. Since its arrival she had dealt with staffing problems by settling a scheduling squabble among the dog walkers; she had written several emails in reply to inquiries for trained bloodhounds; she had eaten her normal lunch of fruit and cheese; and she had stretched out in her recliner and napped for a few minutes.

At seventy-five, Sally was beginning to slow down. She'd lived with a shattered knee for over twenty-five years, and most days she ignored the pain. But those days when she couldn't were getting more frequent. Today was one of them. She reached for her anti-inflammatory pills, knocked over the bottle, trapped it under her hand, and brushed the ivory envelope to the floor.

"Damn!" she mumbled. Sally's pain had grown strong enough to make any irritation seem major. She reached down to pick up the envelope and smacked her hand against the desk leg. "Double damn!" This time she shouted.

In the silence after her outburst, she heard loud chattering and squawking. Sitting back up at her desk, she looked out the window opposite her. There she saw a feathered melee in progress.

The small birdbath had become the focus of King of the Mountain games among the birds in the area. The male robin forced three chickadees and a purple finch to abandon their drinking so that he could bathe. His splashing ablutions were interrupted by a crow. The chickadees, cardinals, and sparrows sat in nearby branches and scolded the bully crow until he flew off in a lazy glide after raising his head for a long last swallow of usurped water.

Sally was entranced. She watched the interplay of the birds intently, cheering for the lone female purple finch. During the height of activity she absently shoved the ivory envelope under a tablet that she'd pulled over to use as an elbow rest. When the birds eventually abandoned their personal pool, Sally's attention was further diverted by a phone call.

"Um, uh, hello?" she stammered into the phone.

Bea responded to Sally's mumbled greeting with a laugh. "Did you forget how to answer the phone?"

"I was watching the birds at the birdbath. Quite a gathering at that little basin."

"Poor things. They're so in need of water. I had a big pileated woodpecker come up under my sprinkler the other day. God, we need some rain!"

"Yeah, we do. And a temp dip to go with it. So what's got you calling in the middle of the day? You're usually much too busy cooking."

"My assistant is cooking tonight. I called to invite you and Belle to dinner with me. It'll be the first time I've ever sat down in the diner and eaten a meal I didn't prepare."

"Your assistant? Who might that be?"

Bea chuckled, "I'll tell all, but at dinner tonight. Say you'll come."

"Yes, I'll come. I can't speak for Belle, though."

"Why not? You usually do." Bea constantly teased Sally about being a ventriloquist and throwing her voice into Belle's mouth.

"Ha-ha!" Sally smiled slightly. "OK, I don't know of anything that Belle has planned for this evening. If she can't make it, we'll let you know."

"No need. Just bring her along if she's available. See you around six."

Sally nodded at the phone, "Bye." She got her good leg in the right position so that she could most easily stand, placed her hands firmly on the chair arms, and stood herself up. She realized with the first step that she had never taken her pain pills. "Oh, well," she muttered, "I guess I can make it to the house."

She walked slowly down the long hall that separated the kennel office from their living quarters – *the house* as opposed to *the office*, even though they were under the same roof.

"Belle, hey, Belle, you back there?" Sally hollered as she walked, tapping the cane down solidly with each step.

"Yes, I'm here."

"We've been invited out to dinner with Bea. And she's not cooking."

A few minutes before six o'clock, Belle and Sally arrived at the Edith Diner. Surprised to see the parking lot nearly full, Belle raised her eyebrows at Sally, whose reply was a shoulder shrug as she said, "I guess we'll see when we get inside."

As she opened the door to the diner, they were greeted by Bea, looking pounds slimmer in seersucker slacks and a loose linen shirt. She was acting as hostess, seating groups of people as they arrived. Ten of the twenty tables were already filled.

Sally glanced at Belle, who again pushed her eyebrows toward her hairline as she muttered, "What in the world?" Her mouth remained slightly open as she stared at Bea. In twenty-five years, she had never seen her friend in slacks.

Bea's smile nearly encompassed her entire face as she sashayed – the only word Sally could come up with to describe the half-dance steps that Bea used to cross the room – toward them. "I saved us a table over here," Bea said with a wink. "Won't you walk this way?"

Sally's eyes sparkled as she grumbled, "I haven't been able to walk that way in twenty-five years. And I didn't know you could either."

Bea chuckled as she seated her friends and reached under the table to pull out a brown paper bag wrapped around a bottle. "Let me open this for you while I help serve. I'll be back in a few minutes." She poured them each a glass of ruby liquid and sashayed back to the kitchen.

Sally raised her glass, toasted Bea's back, and said, "I hope she serves us whatever she's been having."

Belle raised her glass, shook her head, and opened and closed her mouth several times.

"Spit it out. I know you've got something to say."

Belle shook her head slowly and raised an eyebrow, "I can't think of a single word to describe what I'm thinking."

Sally nodded then took another long drink of wine. With a mischievous grin, she leaned over and looked under the table.

"What are you doing?"

"Checking the supplies," she whispered as her head reappeared above the edge of the table. "Thank God, there's another bottle under here."

Belle snorted and took another drink. She picked up the bottle and poured each of them another glass of a very respectable Shiraz. By the time they had sipped half of this round, Bea was back carrying small plates of coleslaw for each of them. She sat at the empty place at the table, poured herself a glass of wine and raised it in salute to Belle then Sally, "Here's to good wine, good friends, and please God, good food!"

Sally was about to explode from curiosity. "Give," she demanded. "Enough pussyfooting. What is going on?"

Bea took a bite of the slaw as she looked back and forth at her friends. "OK, I'll tell you everything in a little while. Let's just eat now. I've still got to serve a few folks, but I have time for this salad first."

She ate quickly then got up and carried plates of food to two tables of people. Finally she arrived back at her table with plates piled high with pork loin, sweet potato fries, and tomato-peach relish. "Now," she mumbled as she tasted the pork. "Pretty darned good."

Belle also took a couple of bites, but Sally only stared at Bea. "If you don't tell me what the hell is going on in the next thirty seconds, I swear I will beat you to death with my cane."

Bea chewed, swallowed, nodded, sipped, and began. "Gerry Krane is going to work for me for a little while. She's cooking tonight for the first time. She needs some money while she's looking for a permanent position, and I need a break."

Belle glanced at Sally who gave a slight shake to her head. Belle nodded slightly before saying, "Looks like you already had a break, a psychic one. Slacks?"

"I know. It's hard to explain without sounding nuts, though."

A warning frown from Sally prompted Bea to keep talking, "When I moved to Plainview and opened this diner, I was only about thirty and looked younger. I figured nobody in this town, then, would trust the cooking of somebody who looked like me. So I changed how I looked. I quit wearing makeup, put my hair in a bun, and chose farm-wife cotton dresses so the real farm wives wouldn't see me as a threat.

"By the time you two moved here I had slipped so totally into that persona that your calling me 'Bea' seemed right. I *was* Andy Taylor's Aunt Bea. And I was okay with that. It's a comfortable role.

"But a couple of months ago I got a catalog in the mail. A clothing catalog. And I fell in love with a pair of red silk pajamas. Definitely not Bea's style."

She stopped for a moment to eat a bite and sip her wine. Belle and Sally merely stared at her. "So I ordered a pair. And started wearing them sometimes after I got home from the diner. Then I ordered other things," she pulled on the collar of her bright turquoise shirt, "like this."

Sally tilted her head to look at Bea's outfit, her lipstick, and her hair gathered loosely into a clip at the back of her neck. "The clothes look great. You look great!"

"I feel great! Like I've broken through a wall I didn't know was there. And it all came to a head yesterday when Gerry asked if I could use some help here at the diner and then I received an expensive-looking envelope addressed in beautiful script to Josephine Murphy. I looked at that envelope and started thinking what kind of woman named Josephine Murphy would receive mail like that. And I got a flash of myself." She sighed heavily, "I never did open that envelope."

Belle narrowed her eyes, "I got an envelope, too. I've been afraid to open it. Afraid there was, I don't know, something official. Or someone looking for me."

Sally gave Belle a worried glance before letting a smile twitch her lips, "I got one, too. It reminded me of my college roommate's wedding invitation. I got to remembering that wedding and forgot to open it. I don't even know where I put it. On my desk somewhere."

Belle deadpanned, "Then you'll never see it again."

The three women laughed at Sally's expense, then went on to finish their dinner and second bottle of wine as they talked of many things. Sally had everyone laughing as she described the incredible wedding of her old roommate, embellishing all the mishaps until it sounded like a Mr. Bean and the Keystone Kops production.

Belle said nothing else about the fears stirred up by the envelope and laughed at all the right places, but Sally noticed the haunted look in her eyes when she let down her guard.

Win was late going in for his dinner. He'd been watering his prize hostas and heucheras. He'd given up on his mother's flowering borders as the shade deepened under the giant oaks with every season's growth. Instead, he'd convinced himself that he preferred the texture and color and shape variations he could get from the mass plantings of colorful and interesting foliage plants.

He had hundreds of hostas, hybridizing his own and field-testing those of other growers. Today he was flying high. He had found a new *sport* of Blue Mouse Ears, the tough little charmer with Mickey-ears for leaves that had been Hosta of the Year a couple years ago. It was times like these when he most missed his mother. Stella Reynolds was an accomplished gardener who would have understood without a word the importance of the little plant with a pale green edge growing among the solid-colored parent plants. It was a spontaneous new variation! Win found it and had nobody to tell.

Win's elation dropped as he realized just how alone he had become. He flopped into his favorite chair and surveyed his comfortable study. No dog on the hearth. No wife in the kitchen. No mother in the garden. He shook himself and said firmly, "I can change this. And I will."

He flipped through the stack of mail he'd carried in with him, glancing disinterestedly at gardening magazines, seed catalogs, news magazines, a couple of bills, and a large ivory envelope. With a shrug and a sigh he laid the mail aside and went to the kitchen to fix himself something to eat. Something substantial and nourishing. His mother had trained him well.

Gerry got home that night tired but energized. She had done it. She'd made it through the first day, cooked a good meal, and pleased Bea. Hell, she pleased herself.

She told Jess all about her day as she threw the ball in the back yard. As she talked about how complimentary Belle and Sally had been, she thought about the book she'd been ready to give up on yesterday. Maybe she could write a little tonight. She wasn't really sleepy yet. Jess seemed to approve as she shoved her head under Gerry's hand for a pat. Gerry was smiling when she came back inside.

She dug through her bag for the notebook where she'd made all her notes during her chats with Sally or Belle. She found it with the ivory envelope jammed into it. She didn't remember putting it there. She impatiently set the envelope aside and carried her notebook to her desk. She flipped through the pages, looking for that Marshal dog. What was his name? Matt?

BellWhether Tails

Dillon – 1964

"Bell, hurry up! Miss Kitty is panting hard and whining." I was smoothing the fur on Miss Kitty's neck and head as she lay panting beside me in the wooden box Gramps had built for just this purpose.

Miss Kitty whined loudly and stood up, pushing as she whined. "Bell, dammit, come on!"

"I'm coming. I can't find the towels we got for the birthing."

"Then get some others and come on! And it's whelping not birthing." Bell refused to learn any of the correct terms for dogs. She didn't know a croupe from the withers, but she was a natural at understanding and communicating with Miss Kitty.

"OK. I'm here." She got on the other side of the whelping box and placed her hand on Miss Kitty's shoulder. "It's okay, girl. It's okay." Miss Kitty relaxed a bit now that Bell was near. She panted and pushed hard again. I reached under her tail to see if the first pup was crowning yet.

"I feel it!" I was trying to act calm but was as nervous about this birthing, er whelping, as Miss Kitty was. I'd been around dogs a lot for the past few years, but I'd never whelped a litter. I'd been reading non-stop from all the dog books I could find at the library and had even borrowed a textbook from Dr. McAdams, our vet. But reading about and doing are two different things.

Miss Kitty gave another push, and I held her first-born in my hands. I broke the sack, tore the umbilical cord, and rubbed the sack off his face with a clean cloth Bell passed to me. "He's not breathing!" I shrieked.

I took a deep breath and remembered the story Louise had told me at the last trial. She had a pup born, not breathing. Flung its head down to dislodge the mucus plug. Yes, that was it.

I took the tiny pup between my palms, raised my arms up in front of my face, and snapped my wrists down. And heard him whine. I opened my hands and saw that the blue cast to the pup's nose was gone. And better, he was squirming and making little sucking noises.

Bell took him from me and laid him at Miss Kitty's side. "Here's your baby, Kit. He's beautiful. You're such a good girl. You did good." She petted Miss Kitty's head as she cooed to her and watched with pride as the new mother cleaned up her son.

I had stopped shaking by the time Miss Kitty delivered the placenta. She ate it quickly then nuzzled her puppy for several minutes.

We watched in wonder.

Finally, Bell looked at me and smiled. "You did good, too."

I nodded. I had.

It took another three hours for Miss Kitty to deliver all six of her pups, four girls and two boys. Bell and I worked out a system where I "received" and she dried them off before giving them to Kit. We were all exhausted and exhilarated when it was over.

Miss Kitty lay back with her six babies each at a nipple. Bell picked up the first-born puppy and examined him carefully. "He looks fine. Good color. No hernia. Breathing sounds good. And look, he has a star on his chest." She pointed to a dark patch surrounded by his white collar."

"I guess he must be a lawman," I said as I stroked his tiny black spot.

Bell nodded. "His name is Dillon."

When the pups were about four weeks old, we introduced them to Thorpe. Their father was interested in them but backed off when they came looking for dinner. Bell laughed at Dillon's insistent searching of Thorpe's belly, "I thought you said he was the smartest of the pups."

I laughed with her but watched the interaction of father and son. Thorpe seemed to accept the nuzzling of Dillon but left when two other pups joined in.

I had claimed Dillon for myself – after all, I had saved his life. I planned to turn him into the best herding dog in America.

Bell had gotten the herding bug when she discovered what a natural worker Miss Kitty was. She and Kit were a well-matched team who had begun to stand out at the trials. I wasn't sure how much I liked that development since they'd outscored Thorpe and me a few times.

She hadn't picked the pup she was going to keep yet. There were two bitches she really liked, and she wavered between them from moment to moment. Annie was slight, fast, and sweet-tempered. Lizzy was bossy, dominant and quick-witted.

Bell and I spent hours watching and evaluating the pups, deciding on what sort of owners each should get. Little Tess, for example, was sweet, pretty and very feminine. We decided she needed a girl in her life, one who'd talk to her and tell her all the secrets she couldn't tell anyone else.

As word got out that my Thorpe and Bell's Miss Kitty had a litter on the ground the inquiries began pouring in. Bell could have sold two dozen of these beautiful pups instead of the four she had available. I looked at the list she'd made of potential buyers. She characterized them with a few words and paired a puppy with each, using many of the criteria that we'd discussed during our puppy evaluations.

"Oh, good. You found a girl for Tess." I looked at the list again, "But you've got people paired up with both Annie and Lizzy?" I frowned my question at her.

"I know. I have to decide. Annie or Lizzy? Lizzy or Annie?"

"Keep them both."

"No. I don't want to try to train littermates together. I've heard too many horror stories."

"Don't keep either."

"That's a possibility. If the buyers are right for them."

"Really?"

She nodded. "You've got Dillon. And we can breed Thorpe and Kit again."

"Yeah. But really? You would really let both those pups go?"

"It would give you a chance to do some winning with Dillon before I bring out my next champion."

"Oh, really? Your motivation is purely altruistic rather than a pitiful inability to decide?"

Bell widened her eyes in an attempt at a look of innocence, "Well, sure."

I shook my head as I walked away. I could come up with no words to convey my incredulity.

As it worked out, Bell did place both Annie and Lizzy. Dillon was the only pup we kept.

I took Dillon to Gramps' ranch with me nearly every day, and Bell and Miss Kitty were usually there, too. She had started working Kit as soon as the pups were weaned.

Dillon was my project, but I found Bell watching me working basic obedience with him. In fact, she was pretending not to watch him the day he first herded a cow.

As a six-month old he had begun following Thorpe to the fields and watching carefully as Thorpe brought home his charges. One day, with no prompting from me, Dillon ran after a straying calf while Thorpe held the rest of the herd together. That began a working partnership that lasted until Thorpe was too old to work.

Dillon learned from watching Thorpe, but he also listened to me. I never had to teach him the same lesson twice. But what impressed me the most was his way of looking to me if he got into a situation he had never before encountered or had difficulty solving.

Once he lost his favorite ball in the creek where it was held in a small pool by a large stick that blocked the water's flow. Dillon tried to get it but the stick was in the way. I told him to get the stick. He did and brought it to me. I said, "Now get your ball." He looked at me carefully, then ran back to the creek and got the ball as it slid over the top of a stone.

When he brought it to me, he crowed in delight, "Woo-roo-woo." That was the first time he used his trademark call.

Bell was at the farm so often she began calling my grandparents "Gran" and "Gramps" as I did. And they looked on her as another granddaughter. Gran even got comfortable ordering her around the way she did me.

"Sally and Edie," Gran refused to call her by her last name – she said it was unladylike – "get your hands washed and get to the table. I didn't cook this stuff to let it get cold."

Bell loved being treated as family. She had none. Adoptive parents dead, no siblings. At dinner that night she announced that Miss Kitty was coming back into season. "Everybody here gets a vote. Should we breed Miss Kitty to Thorpe again?"

I nodded. Gramps did, too. Gran looked thoughtful before saying, "Well, they made pretty babies. No doubt about that. But Edie, you nearly ran yourself ragged running back and forth out here to see to Miss Kitty and the pups." She looked sternly at Bell. "Now I haven't had time to discuss this with Will, but I think if you want to breed her again, you need to move out here while the pups are in the kennel."

Bell looked from Gran to Gramps. Both nodded slightly. "Thank you. I would love to."

My jaw was still dropped. I was talking to myself, urging me not to be jealous, when Bell turned to me. "Is it okay with you, Sally?"

What else could I say?

By the time Dillon was about a year old, I thought he was ready to try a duck trial. Ducks are relatively easy for a young dog to herd. Bell disagreed. She thought I needed to keep training until he could debut on cattle. This became a daily battle as we commuted to the ranch from town each evening that summer. She won.

Dillon's first trial was a triumph. He was nearly perfect. Bell watched him with pride and afterward patted my shoulder and said, "You did good." Then she leaned over Dillon, pounded his side and said, "You, too, boy."

"Thanks! Did you notice anything we need to work on?" I expected a head shake and a smile.

Instead, Bell took out the little notebook she always carried and started ticking off the errors. "You were a little late with the whistle when that heifer swung wide," she began.

I nodded. "Thanks, Coach," I replied none too nicely.

Bell looked at me in puzzlement, then read the next five errors she'd recorded.

I felt like Dr. Frankenstein.

After a few weeks, I let Dillon stay at the ranch with Bell when I couldn't get there for his training sessions. She worked him with Miss Kitty, "Just to keep him in practice," she said. A few weeks more and Miss Kitty was really too pregnant to work. So Dillon got double training, from both me and Bell. She usually stayed out late with him after I drove back to town.

One morning at the office, Bell stopped me with a worried look. "I was out until dark last night working on whistle signals with Dillon, and I got spooked. I felt like somebody was watching me. I didn't say anything to Gramps or Gran because I didn't want them to worry, but I really think someone was out there."

"Did Dillon react?"

"Yes, but he's so obedient he quit growling when I told him to. He kept looking off into the woods though."

"Maybe a fox or a coyote out there."

"No. I really think it was human. I couldn't shake the feeling so I called Dillon in. I stood in the shadows and watched a while but didn't see anything. I was really spooked. Have your grandparents ever said anything about trespassers or, I don't know, watchers?"

"I can't remember that they have. The only thing I remember being strange at all is that Gramps insists that something knocked him off his tractor that time he broke his pelvis. He said he was just mowing like normal when something flew at him and knocked him clean off. Without him to steer it, the tractor ran into a tree and stopped. We all thought he hit the tree and that threw him off, and he just mis-remembered after the shock of the fall and the broken bone. Maybe whatever hit him is stalking you? Werewolf, you think?"

"Don't make fun. It was scary."

"Take Thorpe out with you, too, if you work after dark. And don't call off Dillon next time. The two of them will chase off any interlopers."

"Yeah, OK."

"I'll be out this evening. Might stay over, too, since tomorrow's Saturday. Maybe we should set a trap."

"What kind of trap?" Bell frowned at me.

"I don't know. I'll think on it." I patted her shoulder and went back to work. I had no idea what kind of trap.

I stewed all day about how we could catch the peeper. I asked some of the guys at the sheriff's office if they had any ideas. I even asked Mags Pearson, our font-of-knowledge office manager, if she had any. "Just hide out there and fill his pants with buckshot if he shows his nasty little face."

"That's the problem. He hasn't shown his face. Bell just heard noises and thought he was there."

"Then shoot at the sounds."

"Well, I could. But I might just shoot a deer or coon or something. And how would that look, a deputy hunting out of season? Sheriff would have my butt."

"Honey, you don't seem to notice, but he's been wantin' your butt for a long time." She cackled nastily.

"Mags, you are a dirty-minded old woman," I waved her off as I went back to my desk to stew some more.

I sketched out several plans to trap our peeper. The most complete involved car batteries, trip wires, and head-lights aimed into the woods. Of course it wouldn't work – I had no idea how to set a tripwire.

When I got to the ranch that evening, Bell was waiting for me on the porch. "Did you figure out how to trap the watcher?"

I shook my head sadly. "I've come up with fourteen different ideas and not one of them will work. I guess I'll just follow Mags' advice and sit out there with a shotgun and shoot at any noise I hear."

Bell looked a little sheepish as she stammered a reply, "Um, I, um, did have one idea."

"Really? What?"

"Well, what if we took Thorpe and Kit out to the edge of the woods and put them in a down-stay. You could hide nearby. I'd go on and work with Dillon like I usually do. If you hear anything or sense anything, send the dogs. They can hear and run better than we can. I think they could catch him."

I was dumbstruck. Of course. Use our dogs. It was the obvious solution. I opened and closed my mouth twice, trying to find the right word before I finally croaked, "Right."

Bell examined me for pending sarcasm. "You want to try that?"

I nodded as I went inside to find something to drink. Preferably something stronger than my usual iced tea. "Damn! I am the detective. I should be able to figure this stuff out," I muttered to myself as I looked in the refrigerator for a beer.

"What?" Bell had followed me in, thinking I was talking to her.

"Nothing. Want a beer?" I held up a can of Schlitz, then pressed it to my forehead.

"No, thanks. You okay?"

"Great." I found the opener, pushed in triangle openings on each side of the can, and took a long swallow. "Do you call this thing a church key?" I asked as I brandished the opener in a valiant attempt to change the topic.

"No."

"I've always thought that was a great name for a beer opener. Don't you?"

"Sally, what the hell is wrong with you?"

"Dammit, Bell. I'm supposed to be the detective, good at solving stuff, and you figured out a perfect solution while I was still trying to figure out tripwires."

"Oh. Sorry."

"No. Don't apologize. I'm acting like a jerk. I'm sorry." I took another swallow of the beer. "Let's set up the scene just like you suggested. Maybe we'll catch us a rat."

After dinner, I crept out to the edge of the woods with Thorpe and Kit. I put Thorpe at the right edge of the pasture, Kit at the left edge, and I took the center. I put the dogs into a down-stay, and I ducked into the shadows. Bell came out into the field with Dillon and began working him in obedience commands – down, sit, stay, leave it, take it, and drop it.

After a few minutes, Bell stood still and listened. I looked at Thorpe who was nearer to me than Kit. His ears were pricked and he looked intently into the woods. I signaled to Bell, who gave a big arm-drop, the signal we had agreed on earlier. I released the dogs from their down-stay with a loud "That'll do," followed by "Get him!"

Both dogs tore into the woods, barking and growling. I heard a very human yell followed by loud cursing, an engine starting, and tires spinning. Damn! He had a vehicle parked nearby, probably on the lane just to the south of the woods, over toward J.D.'s place.

I whistled for the dogs. They couldn't outrun a car, and I didn't want them hurt. I walked toward Bell and Dillon and reached them at the same time as Thorpe and Miss Kitty. Thorpe had something in his mouth. I took it and examined it then handed it to Bell: a swatch of denim torn from a pair of jeans with a little blood surrounding the tooth holes.

"Good boy, Thorpe. I hope the bastard has a big hole in his butt." I petted and pounded Thorpe's side.

Bell stroked his head with one hand while petting Miss Kitty's flank with the other. "You are such good dogs. You saved us."

I grinned at Bell as we walked the dogs back up to the house and their kennels, "Now we just have to look for someone with a hole in his jeans and a limp. Piece of cake."

It turned out not to be a piece of cake. We could find nobody that fit my description. I'd even asked the other deputies to keep an eye out for anyone with a noticeably sore thigh or butt.

I was discouraged after a week passed and we'd found nobody. Gramps suggested asking J.D. if he'd seen anyone hanging around his place who might be spying on us. I hadn't seen J.D. in a while, so I decided to take Dillon and walk over to his place right away.

As I neared his house, I hollered a greeting. Gran called that traditional holler a "country doorbell."

J.D. came to the door. When he saw it was me, he stepped out on the porch. "Hey, Sally. Haven't seen you around much lately." He stood near the door, very still.

"Hey, J.D. Listen, we've had a peeping tom over at Gramps' place. Frightened Bell. I wondered if you'd seen anybody hanging around our place or down the lane next to the south end of our woods."

"No. Can't say I have. I'll let you know if I do, though." He gave me the same blank look that usually adorned his face.

"Thanks. I'd appreciate it. Best be getting back now." As I turned to go, Dillon made a low growl. He had planted his feet wide, had his head down and his butt up. He growled again. I started to correct him when I noticed that J.D. was backing up quickly into his house. He bumped his butt on the door handle and grimaced. I looked from him to Dillon, and said quietly, "Well, I'll be damned. Good boy, Dillon."

I walked home praising Dillon with every step. He was a damned good dog. He woo-roo-woo'ed his agreement.

I told Gran, Gramps, and Bell about what happened at J.D.'s. Gran merely nodded. I knew she didn't totally trust J.D. But Gramps was adamant that I was wrong. J.D. wouldn't do that, he swore. I finally stopped trying to convince him but promised myself that J.D. McAllister would not get away with this.

I told the Sheriff and the other deputies about my suspicions. Everyone agreed to help keep an eye out for J.D. If he so much as smiled crooked, we'd haul his butt in for questioning.

J.D. must have gotten wind of my plans. Before I could even get back to the ranch to talk to Gran, J.D. had come over to ask Gramps if he'd keep an eye on J.D.'s place since he had to go to Kansas City on some business. "Business my eye," Gran said when she told me about it. "He's running from you, Sal. Be careful, hon. Cornered animals are mean."

By the time J.D. got back from Kansas City his limp was gone. I had no evidence other than Dillon's growl and my gut.

Bell stayed out of all the discussions I had with Gran and Gramps about J.D. and whether he was capable of such a stunt. She spent some time out in the pasture with the tractor, and asked Gramps to show her exactly where he'd been when he'd broken his pelvis.

"Sally, I have something I want to show you," Bell said to me hesitantly one night after dinner. "Come out to the field with me. I've been working on something."

I got Dillon from his kennel and followed Bell to the field where Gramps had fallen and where she'd been working with Dillon. Bell had parked the tractor there. She also had a ladder leaning against the large oak tree that the tractor had run into. "Come up here, I want you to see something," she said as she climbed the ladder then disappeared into the branches of the tree.

I followed her up the ladder, surprised to see her sitting on a platform a few feet above the bottom branches. "What is this? Did you build it?"

"No. I didn't build it. I found it like this. And I found this, too." She pointed at a piece of rope tied tightly around a limb just below the platform.

"A noose? I never heard of any hangings happening around here."

"I don't think it's a noose. I think it had another use." She pulled the rope onto the platform, tied a longer piece of rope to it, then tied the end of that piece to a large bag of flour. She moved the flour sack to the edge of the platform and motioned for me to come to the edge to look.

She pointed to the tractor below us. She had built a scarecrow and had it sitting in the seat of the tractor. She let go of the flour sack. It swung down and hit the scarecrow in the chest. "I think somebody rigged up something like this to knock Gramps off his tractor. I think there was another line tied between a couple trees at tractor height. When Gramps plowed this row, his tractor hit the line. That tripped a lever that released the weight. And the weight smacked Gramps in the chest, knocking him off the tractor."

I looked over all the parts of the trap and nodded, growing angrier with each nod. "My God. You might be right. It would be tricky, but if someone practiced and set up a guideline for the angle, it could be done. You know what that means? Somebody tried to kill Gramps." As I tried to find a hole in her theory, Dillon began barking furiously.

Someone was walking backward into the woods, his head down so his face couldn't be seen. Dillon pushed him back by advancing toward the intruder, growling with every step. Crouched and snarling, Dillon looked truly frightening. Luckily.

From then on we stopped kenneling Dillon at night. Everyone felt safer with The Marshal on duty.

Three

"A party, like a husband, needs a purpose."
Velma Lee Lewis

"Are you sure you put those invitations in the mail?" Janie looked at her recently delivered mail and saw none of her beautiful little reply envelopes. "I just can't understand it. Nobody has responded to my invitation. Could the entire town be filled with rude people?" She bent double, laid her hands on the floor between her feet, and pushed her back upward. "And my back hurts."

From across the room her aunt looked at her in amusement. "Janie, can you just sit still for five minutes? You're making me nervous." Ruth crossed her ankles on the ottoman, adjusted the pillow behind her back, and looked back to the novel she held in one hand while her other hand fluttered toward Janie.

Janie eyed her aunt with worry. She didn't understand how Ruth could sit hour after hour in her favorite chair with her feet propped up and read. The idea of it was painful to the constantly moving, constantly doing-something Janie. Ruth was overweight, sedentary, and nearing sixty. Janie saw disease and future health problems when she looked at Ruth.

Ruth saw ease and freedom when she thought about herself. She wanted time to sit and read, time to think, time to learn how to knit, although she wasn't sure she wanted to learn to knit. She wasn't lazy; she was weary. Weary of travel, weary of working in the political morass of a large corporation, weary of her old life.

That was why she agreed to move to the back of beyond with Janie. Plainview, Oklahoma, for God's sake.

She still hadn't seen the house Janie bought although she'd seen the photos and videos Janie shot of it. It looked large enough to offer them both some privacy and with a yard large enough to give Jake room to play. She was worried about pale Jake who rarely went outside. He needed to get away from the TV and his computer and into the sunshine. And she thought she was the one to encourage that behavior in the too-smart-for-his-own-good four-year old.

"When did you say your party is going to be? Week after next?" She heard a mumbled reply from Janie's upside-down head. "Well, then, there's still lots of time for RSVPs. Don't fret so." She reached across her book to the table beside her where a bowl of grapes sat gathering moisture from the too humid air. "It's just too damned hot to fret."

Janie arose from the floor in one graceful sweep. Ruth watched her in awe. Oh, to have such a body again. Again, hell. She'd never had such a body, but then she'd never trained for twenty years as a dancer. Nor built up the best dance studio in town before marrying, having a child, and then being left to raise the child alone when Jake's father, Josh or AH as Ruth always thought of him, took off with Janie's assistant.

Unfortunately, Josh's perfidy soured Janie's desire to dance. She sold her dance studio and enrolled in art classes. She had a natural ability to draw that she'd wanted to train for something other than copying cartoon characters on Jake's bedroom walls.

She was good. Her charming Wee Folks caught the attention of an established writer looking for an illustrator for his new children's book. She got the contract, a decent advance, and a share of the royalties. And she immediately got whatever the artist's equivalent of writer's block is called. So she decided to try a geographic cure and move.

"Oh, Ruth, I just thought. I had the RSVPs sent to the new address. No wonder I haven't gotten any." Janie looked so relieved that Ruth nearly laughed.

"Do you need me to do anything to get ready for the movers? My bags are already together so I have time. Want me to pack Jake's room?" Ruth made a half-hearted attempt to stand, slowly, providing Janie ample time to object.

"No, don't bother. I'll get to it in a few minutes. The movers aren't coming until tomorrow morning. Lots of time." Janie was shoving books into a box as she spoke.

Ruth nodded, ate another grape, and looked back at her book. Janie shook her head and looked askance at Ruth. Patience, Janie. Ruth's moving with you to help you out. Don't push your luck.

Just then, galloping footsteps approached from down the hallway. Jake trotted in riding a broom for a horse. "Whoa, there, fella," Ruth said to Jake. "Time to rustle up some chow for cowboys. What does your horsie want for lunch?"

"Oats, Aunt Ruthie. Just oats. And chocolate milk. And peanut butter with strawberry jelly on brown bread. Horsie don't like white bread." Jake's dark curls were plastered to his forehead, his cheeks were rosy, and his blue eyes sparkled. He'd been running Horsie hard through the backyard and around the house at Ruth's earlier suggestion that Horsie could get sick without enough exercise.

Ruth ruffled Jake's hair, swatted his butt, and headed to the kitchen. "Come on, pard, let's get that chow."

Jake started into the kitchen with Ruth, but stopped when he noticed his mother packing books. "Momma, can I get a pony when we move?"

"Jake, we've already talked about that. We won't have room for a horse." She noticed him about to speak and quickly interjected, "Or a pony."

"Well, then, can I have a dog?" He stood looking at her with his eyes pleading.

We'll see, Jakester. We'll see."

Jake darted into the kitchen, "Guess what, Aunt Ruthie. I'm getting a dog!"

Two days later Janie walked through the large dining room of her new house. She hadn't had a formal dining room in her other house and consequently had no furniture. Oh, well, it could be Jake's playroom for now.

There was no space in any of the other rooms for him to play since they were all filled with furniture and boxes. Here at least was an expanse where he could ride Horsie, play with his "men" or simply roll around on the hardwood floors as he was doing just then.

"Momma, there's funny spots on the ceiling. Look." He lay flat on his back in the middle of the room and pointed up at an amoeba-shaped water stain above him.

"I think there must have been a leak in a pipe upstairs some time or other. That's what happens when water gets the plaster wet — it leaves a mark." She lay down on the floor beside him. "You know how we look for pictures in the clouds? Well, can you find any pictures in the ceiling?"

Jake studied the ceiling, glanced at his mother, then looked at the ceiling with a grin. "I think I see a dog up there." He giggled as Janie rolled over and began tickling him.

"You think you can trick me, do you mister? Well, you can't trick me! I'm a lot smarter than I look." They rolled around on the floor, tickling each other and giggling.

Ruth looked in from the doorway to the kitchen. "That would-n't be hard, dear," she said dryly. "You don't look like a rocket scientist rolling around on the floor."

Jake burst into another round of giggles. "Oh, Aunt Ruthie. You're funny!"

Ruth smiled at him and nodded. "You'd better believe it, buster."

He giggled again as she went back to unpacking the dishes into the cabinets. It was easy to be a comic with a giggly four-year-old. But she did used to think of herself as funny. People told her she was. Everyone always enjoyed the stories she told about her travels around the country and the world. Maybe she should try to write some of them down, if she could find the time.

There had been so many things she thought she would do once she "retired" from her corporate position, but now that she no longer had to go to an office, she had trouble accounting for what she did with her days. They simply evaporated into playing with Jake or talking to Janie or some damned thing or another. Was that the way the rest of her life was going to be? Frittered away in dribs and drabs?

"OK, Ruth," she said sternly to herself. "I'm going to put me on a time budget. I'll make a list each morning of what I need to get accomplished that day, then I'll review it and close out items each night. I did it for the corporate jerks I worked for; I can certainly do it for myself. Too bad I didn't start it already. I've actually accomplished something today: unpacking, making Jake laugh, and probably some other stuff."

"Who ya talking to, Aunt Ruthie?" Jake crawled in from the dining room, carrying one of his men – this one a cowboy. His elastic-waisted jeans had ridden down over his hips and his bright orange t-shirt was pushed up under his arms.

Ruth smiled at him. "Just myself. I was giving me a hard time."

"Why? Were you bad?"

Jake's puzzled frown brought a smile to Ruth's eyes. "No, not really bad. Just not very organized. I haven't been getting much done."

Jake stuck his bottom lip out and bunched his brow even tighter. "What do you need to do? You don't have a job. Momma said."

Ruth straightened up with an indrawn breath. "You're right. I don't have a job any more. But I do have one important thing to do." She leaned down and poked a finger in Jake's exposed abdomen. "I have to poke your tummy." She turned the poke into a tickle. Jake was giggling again within seconds.

The doorbell rang. Jake jumped up and ran toward the front door yelling as he went, "I'll get it. I'll get it." He pulled open the heavy door and looked up at the uniformed man standing there. "Are you a po-lice-man?"

Win chuckled as he replied, "Nope. Just the mailman with letters for J.A. Stewart. Is that you?"

"My name is Jake Stewart. And my momma is Janie Stewart. And Aunt Ruth is, um, Aunt Ruth." He stood looking up at the tall expanse of Winston Reynolds. "You're tall."

"Yes, I am. Is your mother at home, Jake?"

Jake nodded vigorously, "Yes."

Win's lip twitched, "Would you go get her, please. Tell her she has mail."

"OK." Jake ran back into the interior of the house yelling, "Momma! You got mail!"

Within a few moments, Janie was at the door with Jake beside her. Jake looked like a miniature version of his mother – same curly black hair, same sparkling blue eyes, same hand-on-hip stance.

"I told ya he was tall, Momma." Janie craned her neck upward until she saw the smiling face of the man in a letter carrier's uniform.

"I'm Janie Stewart. May I help you?"

"I have mail for J.A. Stewart. Could that be you?" Win held out a large hand containing several small ivory envelopes.

She glanced at his offering and blathered, "Oh, yes. That's me. Thank you so much!" She reached out the door, took the envelopes from Win and headed back inside, yelling as she went, "Ruth! Guess what! They RSVPed!"

A few minutes later, Ruth asked the pacing Janie, "How many people did you invite to your party? Jane Ann, are you listening to me? How many invitations did you send?"

Janie pulled at her bottom lip, "I sent one to all the people on this road and all the people in town who own businesses. I think there were thirty-five or forty."

"And how many RSVPs have you received?"

Janie stopped pacing and frowned at Ruth, "I think twenty-five yes and eight no."

"That's great! What a great response!"

"But Ruth, what am I going to serve them? And what am I going to wear?"

"Oh, Janie," Ruth shook her head as she chuckled. "You do beat all." Ruth took two steps toward the back door when Janie called her back.

"Ruth, will you go with me to look at the place I rented for the party? I haven't seen it yet. I found it online and hope it's okay. With this many people coming, I hope it will be big enough."

"Yes, I'll go with you. We'll have to bring Jake, too, of course. But before we go, answer me this: what did you hope to accomplish with this party?"

"I want to meet the folks in town. This seemed like a faster way than the onesy-twosy method of grocery store, gas station, or church, God forbid."

"OK. I can see that. But what are they going to do at this event after meeting you? Are you doing games, music, performance, art? Will you have a buffet or a sit-down meal? I need more information about what you're planning before I can tell you if you have enough space."

"Oh, God. That's a part of the problem. I thought we'd do cocktails and a buffet and I'd wander around and introduce myself and chat with everyone. But you're right. They all know each other, I suppose. This is a tiny town. So what will they do after they've eaten some canapés and scoped us out? Oh, this is going to be a disaster!"

Janie had stopped pacing and was now emoting with large operatic gestures. Ruth thought she'd better intervene before Janie decided to fall on her sword.

"Cut the melodrama and let's think this through." Ruth shifted into her bossy, corporate mode when faced with crisis. "If you were attending this shindig, what would you want to do?" Ruth had a no-nonsense voice she'd used when giving directions or handing out assignments to her staff. She unconsciously slipped into that role as she tried to help Janie sort through her ideas.

Janie pulled at her bottom lip, making Ruth smile – Janie had done that since she was a toddler. "I'd like to get to know my new neighbors and have some fun. And somehow leave an impression of who I am with the new folks. But I don't know how to make that happen." She threw her hands up and paced.

"OK." Ruth took a couple of deep breaths as she looked up at the ceiling of the dining room. "You know, that really does look like a dog," she pointed at one stain next to the door to the kitchen. "A short-legged dog with big ears and a long tail."

"Ruth! I thought you were trying to help me!" Janie had planted her feet wide and her fists on her hips. She leaned forward to get Ruth's complete attention.

Ruth stared at Janie without seeing her. Then she squinted and focused on her niece, "I've got it! A photo booth."

Janie stared at her blankly for several seconds, before a smile slowly spread across her mobile features. "That just might work." She slapped Ruth's palm with her own.

Jake wandered in at that moment, saw his mother and aunt slap hands, and inquired, "Are you playing paddy cakes?"

"No, Jakester. Just giving Aunt Ruthie high fives. She just had a great idea!"

Jake slapped Ruth's hand, "Oh, Aunt Ruthie. You good girl!"

An hour later, Janie pulled up in front of a new-looking building sporting a professionally painted sign that said "Bell-Whether Kennels Training Center."

Ruth studied the building critically before saying, "You rented a dog training building?"

Janie replied softly, "I guess so. It only said it was a large space suitable for parties. Oh, God!" She pulled her lip as she looked from Ruth to the building and back.

"Well, let's go see it. Looks like it's time for lemonade." She unhooked her seatbelt and opened the door.

"Do they have lemonade here, Aunt Ruthie? Good. I'm thirsty." He climbed over the seat to follow Ruth out the door.

Janie sat still. "Wait," she called from behind her hand. "I'm supposed to go ask for someone to show it to us. I'll walk over to the office. Just wait here in the shade, and I'll be right back."

She unbuckled, opened the door, and headed to the office. She seemed to be moving through water or some other more viscous liquid. Jake pulled on Ruth's hand, "Why's Momma moving like that? Is she sick?"

"No, peanut. She's just worried. She'll be fine in a little while." Ruth hoped she was telling the truth to Jake both because she didn't want to lie and because at least twenty-five people were expecting a party that they had to pull off in less than two weeks.

"Where's the lemonade?" Jake shouted to a woman preceding his mother to the building. "Aunt Ruthie said it's lemonade time."

The woman looked puzzled, turning her head to inquire of both Janie and Ruth the meaning of Jake's question.

Ruth responded first, "Oh, I was just using a metaphor..." she drifted off into a mumble, aware of how her slight would sound to the owner of the building.

Belle nodded. "Ah." She opened the door and stood aside, waving first Janie, then Ruth and Jake inside.

Ruth watched Janie's reaction carefully. She saw no start of horror, no wilting with future embarrassment. Reassured, she stepped inside and looked around. She saw a large room with shining oak floor and white walls. It was clean and bright, if not decorated. Hmm, not bad. We can work with this space. She caught Janie's eye and tried to telegraph her relief.

Janie sighed audibly. "This is very nice," she said aloud. She took another couple of breaths before continuing. "We have the place rented for the Saturday evening, but how much earlier than that could we get in for set-up and decoration?"

"After noon on Friday it will be available." Belle was still amused at this young woman's reaction. Did she think the place would be filled with dog crates?

"Oh, yes. That will be fine. And I do hope you'll be able to attend."

Belle looked surprised. Had she been invited? Janie held out a bundle of small ivory cards to her aunt, and the penny dropped. Lord, the ivory envelope. She'd never opened it. What the hell had she done with it? "Um, yes. I think, um, I was checking on some, um, conflicts...." She let her own voice drift off. "Stay as long as you'd like. Just lock up and bring me the key when you're done," she said with much more certainty as she brushed her hair off her forehead.

When she turned to walk away, Janie jumped into the air and clicked her heels. Ruth, used to these spontaneous eruptions, did not react. Belle, on the other hand, gasped then grinned as she walked back to the office. This new blood looked like a welcome infusion into the staid and stagnant social life of Plainview.

Four

"Never remind people of past errors or present pleasures."
Velma Lee Lewis

"Sally! Sally!" Belle began hollering before she had the door to the office fully closed. She looked in the storeroom, poked her head into the kennel area, and moved quickly to the hallway to their living quarters. "Sally? Are you back there?"

"What? I'm in the kitchen." Sally's voice was indistinct, almost mumbled.

"Are you eating again? I thought you wanted to lose weight." Belle rounded the corner into the kitchen and caught Sally with a cookie on its way to her mouth.

"Whatever." Sally wiped her mouth. "Surely you weren't bellowing at me over a cookie you didn't know I was eating." Her eyebrows raised one at a time.

"No, I was calling you for something else. Do you know about a party that we're invited to in two weeks in our training building?"

Sally shook her head. "No. Are we having a party in two weeks? I didn't know about it. What's it for? And are *you* putting it together?" Sally fired questions at Belle, the last accompanied by unfeigned confusion.

"Oh, of course I'm not putting together a party. That young woman, Janie something, has rented it for a party. And she said she hoped I was attending. I think she sent us invitations, but I don't know what happened to them. Ivory envelopes?"

"I don't know. I never opened mine. Where did I even put it?" Sally got up and started to the door, knocking her cane off the chair back as she did. "Damned cane. You'd think I'd get used to it after twenty-five years."

"I don't know what I did with my invitation either. Now we'll look very rude. We didn't even have the grace to respond." She thrust her hands upward, snapping her wrists as her palms turned ceilingward.

Belle's distress was so melodramatic that Sally chuckled. "Why are you so exercised over this? It's not that big of a deal, is it?"

"I don't know. Just seems I'm starting to let things slip…" She looked questioningly at Sally.

"Oh, you're fine. You're still the most organized person I know." Sally smiled at Belle in what she hoped was a reassuring way.

"That's not saying much!" Belle snapped.

Sally grinned and made her way to the office to hunt for the lost ivory envelope.

As she reached her desk, the phone rang. She snagged it with one hand while the other shuffled through the layers of papers of her "I know where everything is" stacks. "Damn," she shouted into the phone as a jumble of papers hit the floor. "I mean, hello." She tried unsuccessfully to hold the phone while leaning to the floor to retrieve the dropped papers. The phone bounced onto the papers and skidded across the floor. "Double damn!" She hooked the phone with her cane and pulled it within reach. "Sorry. Sorry. Hello?"

"Sally? Are you okay?" Bea's voice on the other end of the line sounded concerned.

"I'm fine. Just knocked off a stack of papers and dropped the phone." Sally continued to shuffle through her papers, exclaiming, "Got it."

"Got what? Are you sure you're okay?"

"Oh, I misplaced an invitation to a party and never sent an RSVP. Belle yelled at me about it. I found it now. So what's up?"

Sally tore open the ivory envelope and extracted a printed invitation and a small card and envelope as she spoke.

Bea sighed. "Crap. I haven't sent in my RSVP either. That new artist is going to wonder what kind of rude place she moved to."

"You didn't call about that, though. What's up?" Sally marked the *I WILL attend* box on the reply card as she spoke.

"I wondered if you would board Shep for me for a few days. I want to make a trip, and it's too hot to take him with me."

Sally's eyes widened. "A trip? You? Are taking a trip?"

Bea laughed, "I just keep surprising you, huh?"

"Sure do. A trip? Really? When? Where?" Sally's interrogation technique had always been staccato.

"When? In a couple weeks. How long? Maybe a week. Where? Central Arkansas. And before you ask, why is my business, although I'll probably end up telling you when I get back."

"OK."

"OK, what? OK, you'll keep Shep or OK, you'll quit quizzing me?"

Sally chuckled, "OK to both. Just let me know when you're leaving and we'll get a run ready for Shep. Don't worry about him. He'll be fine."

"I know he'll be fine. I'm wondering if I will."

"Can't help you there. But I'm happy to listen whenever you want to talk."

"Thanks, Sal. You're the best. I'll let you know when I have something to say. On another topic, Gerry's really doing good work at the diner. Before long she'll be able to run the place without me."

Sally frowned, "Is that what you're planning? Letting Gerry run the diner for you? Then what would you do?"

"Don't worry. Gerry doesn't want to run it for long, and I don't want her to. But the freedom to leave for a while is something I've missed for years. Even beloved businesses can easily turn into traps, can't they?"

Sally nodded, thinking about how long it had been since either she or Belle had been away from the kennel for more than a few hours for anything other than dog shows or trials. "Yeah, they can. Golden handcuffs."

"Maybe you two need to figure out how to take off your handcuffs, too."

"Yeah, I suppose we should. But we'd have to find someone to run the place if we left."

"Well, you can't have Gerry. She's taken."

"For now," Sally shot back.

"Anyway, thanks for being willing to board Shep. I'll get back to you with dates."

"No problem, Bea. Or should I say Josephine?"

"Maybe. I'll let you know about that, too." Bea found herself smiling at the thought of leaving Bea behind.

After hanging up, Sally stuffed her reply card into its envelope and dropped it in the outgoing mail basket by the door. Bradley, one of the kennel kids, would drop it by the post office in Edith when he picked up the incoming mail this afternoon. Sally thought she'd keep quiet about sending back the reply card until Belle reminded her. Then she could crow that she'd already done it. She'd learned long ago to enjoy the small pleasures when she found them.

Bea sat next to the phone for several minutes after disconnecting. Sally raised a good question: what name did she want to use?

She practiced calling herself Josephine and Jo. She thought she'd opt for Jo – she'd been Jo for a while before she moved to Plainview. Once here, she'd been Josephine until Sally rechristened her Bea. Before that, her mother had been the primary one to call her Josephine, and then only when angry.

She'd solidified her travel plans by talking about them with Sally. Until she actually said the words she'd had trouble believing that she was going back to Arkansas. And more trouble still imagining what she'd find there.

Thirty years changed things: people, circumstances, relationships. She'd almost convinced herself that she was ready to face whatever or whoever awaited her.

A knock sounded at her door, jarring her back to the present. Puzzled, she went to answer it, shushing Shep's barking as she went. When she opened the door, she stepped back in surprise. A middle-aged woman she didn't know stood on the porch.

"Are you Bea Murphy?" asked the woman with a smile. At Bea's nod she continued, "I'm so sorry to bother you at home, but I couldn't find a phone number for you and the woman at the diner told me where you lived."

Bea nodded again, "What can I do for you?"

The woman wiped the back of her hand across her brow, "Do you mind if I come in? I really can't deal with this heat."

Bea opened her door wider and motioned the woman into the living room.

Once the woman was seated she began to explain, "My name is Ruth Welborne. I've just moved to Plainview with my niece, Janie Stewart, and her son. We live just down the street in the large yellow house."

She took a breath as she wiped her hand across her forehead. "Janie is throwing a 'getting to know you' party a week from Saturday. She's rented a space from BellWhether Kennels. She's sent out invitations and has at least twenty-five acceptances. What she hasn't done is arrange for anything to eat at this party. Four different people referred me to you as the best cook and caterer in the area. I've come to beg you to help us out on the short notice and supply us with canapés and appetizers for the party."

During Ruth's recitation, Bea studied her closely, listening to her words but watching her facial expressions and body language carefully as well. She saw bright blue eyes under trifocals, a smattering of freckles, graying blond hair and a pug nose. She heard the slight bossiness in Ruth's tone and her Midwestern vowels, and noticed her fingers tapping on her knee as she spoke.

A slow smile drifted across Bea's face. She slightly shook herself before saying, seemingly out of nowhere, "Did you graduate from high school in Conway, Arkansas?"

Ruth's head jerked in surprise, "Well, yes I did. In 1970. Why?"

The smile engulfed Bea's face, "I graduated from there in 1969. People knew me as Josie Murphy then."

Ruth's jaw dropped. "Really? Josie Murphy? Really? My God! Really?"

Bea nodded repeatedly, "And Ruthie Welborne? In Plainview, Oklahoma! I'm amazed. I thought I'd heard you moved to New York or Chicago or somewhere."

"Yeah, I did. Chicago. I lived there for about thirty-five years. I worked for AFCO for twenty-seven, selling IT services and software to large financial institutions. I just retired from there a couple months ago. Janie decided to move here to work on her book and invited me along." She stared at Bea/Josie, looking for the girl she'd known in the woman sitting across from her. "I just can't get my head around your being Josie and being here."

"I know. What a surprise. And what a nice one! We'll have to have a long visit and catch each other up on what we've done with forty years. But first, let me respond to your initial inquiry: yes, I will do the catering for your party. I'll get you a rate sheet and you can select your menu from that."

"Oh!" Ruth exhaled loudly. "Thank you! I didn't know what we'd do if you refused."

Bea walked to her desk, found her rate sheet, and handed a copy to Ruth. "I'll need your order by Wednesday."

Ruth glanced at the sheet and nodded. "I'll get Janie to make her selections, and I'll get back to you." She stood, "I won't take any more of your time right now, since I just barged in on you. But I do want us to get together for a long talk very soon." She held out her hand to Bea.

Bea took Ruth's hand then pulled her close for a hug. "I am so happy to see you again. Let's try to set up time to talk when you get back to me with your menu. My phone number is on the rate sheet. Damn! Ruthie Welborne living down the street from me in Plainview, Oklahoma. Who would ever believe it?"

Ruth promised a call within two days and departed with another hug. "Plainview had better watch out now that there are two Wampus Cats in town!" She walked out of the house whistling the school song.

Janie's reaction to Ruth's news was not unexpected. "You're kidding! You went to high school with the caterer?" Janie's hands, uncharacteristically still, remained on her hips. "But she did say she'd do the catering, didn't she?"

Ruth smiled, "Yes, Janie, she'll do the catering." She shook her head, "I am still amazed that you forgot to arrange for the food. It's not like you."

Janie threw her hands up until they flapped around her ears. "I know. I guess I just got ahead of myself with moving. I should have waited until we were moved in and settled." She sighed heavily. "Thank you for helping me out."

Ruth examined her niece. Janie's charcoal-smudged hands dropped to her sides. She looked tired. "Have you been working this morning? Did you make any progress on the set of drawings due next?"

Janie took deep breaths as she shook her head. "No. I can't seem to get the drawing right. My Wee Folk all look deformed rather than small and interesting. Oh, Ruth, I thought that moving here would be good for me. I'd have quiet, a bright studio, room for Jake to play, and none of the distractions of Josh or Marla or my old life. But it's just the same. The noise is in my head."

"One day is probably not a real good test. You might want to ease into it. Let's get the party over, then you'll be able to concentrate on setting up your studio and getting your mind back on your work."

"Right." Janie moved her eyes from Ruth's calm face to the rate card in her hand. "There's a good selection here. Let's see, how about stuffed cherry tomatoes and bacon-wrapped asparagus?"

"It all looks good. Just make a list. Then I'll get back with it to Josie. On another note, did you find a photo booth to rent?"

Janie looked at Ruth, "Do you like California rolls or Swedish meatballs better?"

Ruth handed Janie a pad of paper and a pen as she walked out of the room. "Just make a list. I've got to go Google."

Janie called after her, "Is your throat sore? There's mouthwash under my sink."

Ruth came to a halt and turned back to look at Janie who was writing furiously. "I said *Google*," she muttered.

After several minutes with her favorite search engine, Ruth placed a call to a supplier in Enid who appeared to have exactly what she wanted. "So you can deliver the photo booth between noon and six o'clock next Friday evening? That's the thirteenth. What? No, I don't think Friday the Thirteenth is particularly unlucky. You'll bill it to the credit card, right? Please call when you're within thirty minutes of delivery and I'll meet you at the site. Very good. Thank you." Ruth hung up and finished making notes.

"Janie, you around?" she yelled down the hallway.

"In the kitchen."

Ruth carried the notepad with her as she walked purposefully toward the kitchen. Just as she reached the door to the dining room, a small voice demanded, "Stick 'em up, lady." A tousled head partially covered by a red bandana stood in front of her, pointing a water pistol at her belly.

"Ohh!" she jumped backward in surprise, delighting the miniature robber in the doorway.

"Did I scare ya, Aunt Ruthie? It's just me, Jake." He pulled the bandana off his nose and mouth. "I won't hurt you. Really!"

"Jake. You did scare me." Her hand went automatically to ruffle his curls. "You need to be careful scaring old ladies. We could get hurt."

"Aunt Ruthie, you're not old. You don't walk with a stick. Or take your teeth out."

"That's how you tell, huh?" Ruth chuckled as she bent to look Jake in the eye.

Jake patted her on the cheek. "I think you're just a little old." He reached a finger under her glasses and touched the skin at the outer corner of her eye. "Your eyes are old," he pronounced with a firm nod, patted her cheek again, and left her still bent double in the doorway.

"Did you drop something?" Janie called from the sink as she noticed Ruth looking at the floor.

"No, just recovering from being told that I have old eyes." Ruth lifted an eyebrow.

Janie grinned. "Did your old eyes find a photo booth?"

"Yep. Be delivered between noon and six on the thirteenth. With supplies. Enough for a hundred strips of four photos."

"That's great. Thank you for doing that. Now I just need something to put the photo strips in. Some sort of scrap book, I guess, with room for the person's name and a comment."

"I'll look for one tomorrow. I'm going into Ponca City to see what services and shops are there. And I'll see if I can find something to hold a strip of photos for the guests to take home."

"That's a great idea. You're wonderful. One more thing: will you man the booth at the party?"

"No, I will not *man* the booth at the party. Do I look like a man? I will *staff* the booth." She turned to leave, then whirled back. "Jane Ann! I am ashamed of you!" She walked to her office mumbling, "You young women have forgotten how hard it was for us to get you the rights you now just assume are yours. I don't know what's going to happen…"

Janie jumped from foot to foot softly repeating, "Yes, yes, yes!" She loved to get Ruth worked up into a feminist frenzy.

Five

"For a summer buffet serve two meats, four savories, three sweets, and yellow punch."
Velma Lee Lewis

Ruth surveyed the party room. Tables borrowed from the Edith Public School were covered with inexpensive tablecloths she'd found online. Chairs also from the school were lined up at the tables and along the wall. The buffet line was set up awaiting the food Bea would bring. The flowers had been delivered and strategically placed around the room. The bar in the corner was stocked. Bradley, the helpful kid who worked at the kennel, would play bartender. He swore he knew how to mix drinks even though Ruth assured him that serving soft drinks, beer, and two colors of wine didn't require a mixology license.

Even the star of the party, the photo booth, had arrived on time and was working properly when Jake took a strip of photos of his feet.

Ruth only needed to get her face made up and her clothes changed. Where was Janie? She promised to be here in ample time for Ruth to get ready. Then Janie could take care of the last-minute stuff. This was supposed to be Janie's party, after all.

She paced around the perimeter of the room, hunting for Jake as she recounted chairs. Forty should be enough. Didn't Janie say she had thirty-three acceptances? As she stopped to check out the room from the back, she felt fur cross her foot. She kicked forward and connected with something soft – Jake.

"Oh, God, Jake! Did I hurt you? You scared me. I thought you were a mouse." Jake rolled back onto the floor, pulled his knees up to his chest, and made moaning sounds. "Oh, no! Did I kick you in the stomach? Are you okay? Jake?" She bent down to examine the small boy lying at her feet when she realized he wasn't moaning but laughing.

She plopped down on the floor beside him. "Jakester, I'm going to get you! You, you, you little pill!" She grabbed his knees and spun him around so that he whirled out into the center of the room. His giggling increased in volume as he slowed to a stop.

"Do it again, Aunt Ruthie!"

"I shouldn't have done it once! Stand up and let me look at you. If you're all dirty, you'll have to go home when I do and put on clean clothes. Your mother will have a fit. You can't come to the party dirty." Ruth pulled him to his feet and turned him around so she could look at his back. "Whew! We got lucky. You're still clean."

Jake leaped into the air with a wild cheer. "Yay! I don't need to change clothes. Yay! I'm clean! I'm clean!" He ran in widening circles yelling "I'm clean!" until he crashed into the khaki-covered legs of Bradley King.

"Whoa, there, buddy." Bradley lifted Jake up to look him in the face. "What are you yelling?"

Jake was struck dumb, hanging with his feet dangling above the ground. After a few seconds he said in a tiny voice, "I'm clean."

"You're clean?" Bradley frowned from Jake to Ruth who by now had hoisted herself off the floor and made her way to the front of the room.

"Yes. He's clean. He won't have to change his clothes again before the party. Maybe if you hold him up off the ground he can even stay out of trouble until his mother gets here." She swatted Jake's butt as she walked past him. "Stay clean."

"But I want down," Jake mumbled. Then he tucked his chin into his neck and looked up at Bradley from under long dark lashes. "Please."

Bradley winked and set him down. "OK, bud. Why don't you help me get the cokes in the tub of ice. And don't get dirty. I don't want to get in the doghouse with your mother."

Jake stared up at Bradley in wonder. "Why would my momma want to get in a doghouse with you? And where's a doghouse? I heard some dogs barking but I don't see their house. Can I go look for it? I'll see if my momma's in it."

Ruth grinned at Bradley. "See what you started?" She dropped a hand on Jake's head. "Take it down a notch, Jake. Your momma's not in a doghouse. Bradley just meant he didn't want to be in trouble. It's just an expression."

"Well it's a silly spreshon. Momma doesn't get in dog houses!" He turned indignant eyes back to Bradley. "My momma lives in a people house!"

Bradley's chest raised and lowered under a heavy sigh. "OK, Jake. I'm sorry. Let's go put the ice in the tub."

Jake, torn between indignation and curiosity, stood indecisively for a few seconds until Ruth's pat on his back sent him scurrying after Bradley. "How much ice will we need? Will it be cold? Won't it melt? Why are we putting it in a tub? How many cokes do we need to put in it?"

Bradley tried valiantly to lob responses between the barrage of questions but gave up when it became obvious that Jake was more interested in the questions than the answers. He looked across the room to Ruth who was watching the interaction with interest. "Is he always like this?"

She nodded. "Yes. To one degree or another. He's especially wound today because of the party."

"What do you mean I'm wound, Aunt Ruthie? I'm not wound. I'm clean. You said." His head popped up at the back of the bar. He looked for Ruth, but saw Janie instead. "Momma! Am I wound?"

Janie took a few steps into the room, "I would say so!" She looked around, noticing the flowers, the seating, the table decorations. "It looks wonderful, Ruth. You've pulled off a miracle." She gave her aunt a bear hug. "And guess what? After you guys left the house, I had an idea for one of the paintings I'm working on. I sketched it out and I like it. That's why I'm late. Sorry."

"Don't be sorry if you broke down that wall. I'm so glad you got something you like. That must be a good omen. This is going to be a good party. I'll be back as fast as I can." She hurriedly left the room as Janie introduced herself to Bradley.

"Sally! Aren't you ready yet? It's time to go over to the party." Belle looked cool and crisp in tan linen slacks and a peach cotton shirt with matching coral earrings and beads. "I hope I'm not dressed too casual, but it's too damned hot to be fussy."

Sally's cane announced her entrance into the kitchen. "You look fine. Will I do?" She turned around slowly, showing off her pale blue tunic over navy slacks. Her long white braid was pinned to the back of her head in a French twist.

Belle cocked an eyebrow, "You clean up pretty good."

"What time are we supposed to be at this thing?"

Belle picked up the invitation, looking at it carefully, as if she hadn't looked at it fifteen times today. "It starts at five. Odd time, don't you think? I suppose it's just going to be cocktails, not dinner, but folks around here eat early. I bet most of them will be expecting a meal."

"You're probably right. But from what Bea says, there'll be enough food for everyone. I wonder if she's here yet. Maybe we should go on over and make sure everything's okay."

"No, we're guests. And Gerry will be there to help Bea."

"They're guests, too. Town this size, everybody plays worker and guest all the time." Sally smoothed the wrinkles from her tunic. "Why does cool fabric have to wrinkle so badly?"

"I don't know. Never thought about it."

Sally sat down at the table and pulled the invitation to her. "She sure printed up some fancy invitations for a party at a kennel."

Belle stiffened. "There's nothing wrong with that space. I think it will work well as a party room." Belle had pushed for them to build the training facility. She was rightly proud of how it added to the income of the kennel through charging for classes and now for the space itself.

"Oh, calm down. I was just thinking that when I saw that invitation come in the mail, I had imagined it had something more grand than a party at our kennel to announce."

Belle agreed, "Me, too. I was afraid it was some official inquiry. Someone looking for me." She looked searchingly at Sally.

"Oh, Belle. You must have been frightened. Why didn't you say anything to me?" Sally's worried gaze focused on Belle.

"I was being silly. Nobody's likely to come looking for me after all these years." She took a deep breath. "I guess it's time to go." She patted Sally's shoulder as she walked past her. "Thanks."

"For what?"

"Understanding. You're the only person in the world who does."

Sally nodded grimly. Sadly, she thought, that's true.

"Gerry, would you go back out to the car. I must have left the bowl of melon balls out there." Bea busily loaded serving dishes with food from the containers she'd brought in.

Janie watched the activity with rising panic. It was nearly five o'clock, Ruth had not returned, and no guests had arrived. She'd figured this little town for being early with everything. "Do you think people will be here soon?" she asked Bea.

Bea nodded, "Um-hmm. Everyone will arrive together at about 5:16."

"Really? Why's that?"

Bea's eyes twinkled as she remembered the story. "Until the year when she died, Miss Velma Lee Lewis was the grand doyenne of etiquette in Plainview and Edith. Whatever she said about how things should be done was taken as gospel. Apparently, she once gave a party to which all the guests arrived early. She was still in her hairpins and was mortified that she had been seen so. A few weeks later, she wrote a letter to the editor of the little weekly paper that used to be published in Edith. She said that no self-respecting guest would ever arrive at a party earlier than a quarter hour past its start. Everyone believed her."

Janie laughed. "I'd have liked to meet her."

Bea agreed, "She was a character. Feisty but proper and prissy until the day she died. Made her niece promise to bury her in her white gloves."

"You made that up!" Janie spouted.

"Nope. Ask anybody. In fact, do ask anybody. It would be a good ice-breaker. Everybody has Miss Velma Lee stories. And they love to tell them."

"What a great idea. Thank you. I'm glad to finally meet you. Ruth has spoken of you several times. She's so pleased to find you here. I think she was afraid there'd be nobody here for her to befriend."

Bea finished spooning the melon balls that Gerry had brought to her into the final empty bowl. She glanced at her watch. "Five more minutes." She gathered up all the boxes and containers she'd brought and hid them under the skirted tables of the buffet line. "I'm tickled that Ruth's here, too. We haven't had the chance to really catch up yet, but we will. Soon." She looked up to see Ruth coming in the door and smiled at her.

"The parking lot is filling up with cars, but nobody's getting out of them. Are they waiting for something? It's nearly a quarter after."

Bea and Janie laughed as Ruth looked puzzled.

"I'll tell you later," Janie promised. "Let's go stand near the door. They'll all be coming in a minute."

Ruth followed Janie to the door after detouring by the bar to round up Jake, wet to his elbows and dripping on the floor. "Good grief! Jake, I thought you weren't going to get dirty."

"I ain't dirty, Aunt Ruthie. Ice ain't dirty. It's *clean*." He shouted the final word just as the door opened to reveal a long line of the guests of the party.

"I'm collecting Miss Velma Lee stories," Janie announced to the group of five women standing near the punchbowl. "I've only heard of her today, but I'm intrigued. Can anybody add to my collection?"

The women looked at each other and laughed. The eldest in the group, a wizened octogenarian with wispy hair pulled into a tight bun, pushed her wire-framed glasses up her nose with a gnarled forefinger. "You want stories or sayin's?"

Janie shrugged slightly. "I don't know about sayings. What are they?"

A younger version of the first speaker said, "Tell her some of the sayin's, Momma. That'll give her the idea."

"All right, Betsy, let me think." She looked at the ceiling for a few seconds before breaking into a smile. "Only spit in moving water or deep leaves," she proclaimed.

The other women chuckled, but Janie looked blank. Betsy said, "I think we hit her with it too fast. Let me see if I can explain. You'uns correct me if I misspeak."

Amid reassurances that they wouldn't let Betsy leave out anything important, Betsy took a deep breath and began her story. "Miss Velma Lee Lewis lived in Plainview her whole life except for a few years in St. Louis at the..." she paused, raised her hands conductor style, and led the others to intone sonorously, "...Mansfield Finishing School for Young Women."

She grinned at Janie before continuing. "You can see we're all familiar with this story. Anyway when she returned to Plainview after her finishing, she came with the expectation of finding a husband. Her father was the only doctor in the county. His daughter was a good catch. Under normal circumstances she would have had her choice of suitors, but she had the unfortunate luck of looking for a husband in 1917, when all the eligible young men were in Europe or cemeteries.

"She didn't find a husband. Ever. She ended up living with her parents until they died, then living in their house until she died in 2003, at age 103.

"During her long tenure in this town, she attempted several enterprises, but the only successful one was an etiquette school, Miss Thelma Lee's School of Manners. She convinced all the mothers in town that their children could not succeed without good manners. And she spent the rest of her life spelling out the do's and don'ts of those manners.

"Thus the *sayin's*." Betsy took a long swallow of her beer and looked at the others. "What did I forget?"

General murmurs of "Nothing" and "You did fine" came from the women. One, a tall, slender, stern-faced woman of about seventy-five added, "We had to keep a notebook where we wrote down all her rules, or sayin's. I think I still have mine."

Janie was delighted. "Oh, I'd love to see it. Tell me either a story or a sayin'. Help me know this remarkable woman."

Betsy spoke first, "My favorite is 'Never look an older man in the eye.'" She laughed, "I've spent forty years trying to understand what could have prompted that edict."

"Always put on your right shoe first," said a short plump woman with an infectious smile.

"Never dust your tabletops after sunset," the final woman added.

"Wow!" Janie looked around the room. "Do you think everyone here knows a sayin'?"

Betsy's mother looked over the guests. "Anybody who grew up around here that's over twenty-five would." The others nodded agreement.

"Even the men?" Janie asked.

The tall thin woman replied, "Most of the boys got sent to etiquette class, too. And even those who had to work at home would have heard at least some of the sayin's from their mothers, sisters, and friends."

Janie stared unseeing at the wall across from her. Finally she focused on Betsy's mother. "I've got an idea." She looked at the other women again and said, "I'm sorry. Would you tell me your names again?"

Betsy stuck her hand up in the air quickly, "Betsy King. My son, Bradley, is tending bar. This is my mother, Abigail Adams – she married the name – called Miss Abby by everyone in town but my sister and me. She taught most of them."

The tall thin woman held her hand up next, "Sylvia Pope. I teach in Edith where Betsy's the principal."

The other two women were also teachers, Brenda Sue O'Connell and Marge Dunlap. After repeating each name and thanking them again for coming to her party, Janie left the circle and moved to the center of the room.

"May I have your attention, everyone! First of all, thanks to all of you for coming out on this hot afternoon. I'm so happy to meet you all. Now my family and I can begin to feel a part of Plainview.

"We had planned to ask each of you to visit the photo booth in the corner and shoot a strip of photos of yourself. Then paste your strip in my scrapbook and write your name next to it. You can shoot an extra strip to take with you if you like. There are cards available for that. Then you can send your card to a sweetheart, a grandchild, or an old friend." She paused to let the chuckles subside.

"As I said, that's what we had planned. And we'd still like you to do that. But I have an additional request after learning about Miss Velma Lee today. Would each of you also write beside your picture your favorite Miss Velma Lee sayin'. That'll help us get to know you and Miss Velma Lee at the same time."

This time the laughter was more prolonged, and Janie had to attempt to speak twice before it quieted. "From what I've heard, we need to understand Miss Velma Lee to understand Plainview."

Several voices responded, "You can say that again," and "Boy, howdy!" Finally a stooped, once-tall man in a striped Western-cut shirt and jeans stepped forward. "Honey, I lived next door to Miss Velma Lee for over seventy years. Anything you want to know, you just ask me."

Janie made a show of looking slightly away from him as she intoned, "Never look an older man in the eye."

Everyone was having fun, telling Miss Velma Lee stories and sayin's to Janie, Ruth, and each other, and taking photos of themselves, alone or in groups, then pasting them in the scrapbook.

Suddenly, the outside door flew open and a very tall, very dirty man stormed in yelling, "Bea! Bea Murphy! Are you in here?"

Bea ran out from behind the buffet table with Gerry on her heels. Gerry shouted, "Smoke! Over here!"

Win turned toward Gerry's voice as Bea nearly crashed into him. "What's wrong Win? You look frantic," Bea put a calming hand on Win's arm as Belle and Sally rushed up to join the group.

Win wiped a dirty hand across his sweaty, smudged forehead. "Thank goodness I found you. I tried to call you at the diner and got no answer. I tried to call the kennel and got no answer. In fact, I tried to call nearly every damned person in town." He stopped and looked around. "And they're all here." He looked back to Bea in wonder, "What is this?"

"It's a party, Smoke. Given by the new family in town, Janie Stewart and her aunt, Ruth Welborne. Why didn't you come?" Gerry demanded. Then moving a step away from him after taking a big sniff, she said, "You smell like smoke!"

Win took a deep breath. "That's what I'm trying to tell you." He took Bea's hand in his large dirty one, "There was a fire at your house. In your kitchen. I put it out, got Shep out, and left him at my house. I've been looking for you ever since."

Bea's other hand flew to her mouth, "My kitchen burned? Shep's okay? Are you sure? You put out the fire?"

Win nodded to each question. "I was home this afternoon — it's my day off — reading, when I decided I needed to turn the sprinkler on a new bed I planted. As soon as I stepped outside, I could smell the smoke." He paused to breathe then continued, speaking quickly. "I traced the smoke to your house and saw flames in the kitchen window when I got close. I opened the front door, called to Shep, who came out whining, found your garden hose, and tackled the fire.

"It looked like a towel caught on fire from a burner left on. The towel had wicked up some spilled olive oil on the counter. It made a pretty good flame. Luckily the tile countertop didn't burn, so the flames were contained to the oily towel. The damage to the kitchen is mostly from the smoke. And the water I shot in through the window." He looked sheepish, "Turns out I didn't need to do that."

"Oh, Win! Don't apologize for goodness sake. You saved my house. And my dog!" Bea burst into tears. Win gave her a hug while Belle and Sally patted her back.

Gerry grinned at Win. "Good thing you were home. But I still don't understand why you were. Why didn't you come to the party?"

"I didn't know about it."

"I know Janie sent you an invitation. I saw the guest list. Maybe it got lost in the mail. I hear the mailman's not very reliable." She reached up and patted his cheek as Janie and Ruth arrived.

"Is everything okay, Josie?" Ruth asked. Belle, Sally and Gerry looked surprised. Josie?

Bea wiped her eyes and smiled, "Thanks to the quick thinking of this young man. Win saw smoke at my house, put out the fire, and saved my house and dog." She burst into tears again.

Janie said quietly, "Thank goodness you were home. I was going to be angry at you for not responding to my party invitation, but it looks like your being home was providential."

Win blushed. "I didn't know about the party. I guess the invitation didn't arrive or I misplaced it. I'm sorry. I would have come."

Janie raised an eyebrow, "Don't apologize." She gave him an appraising look from the tips of his dirty tennis shoes to the top of his disheveled head. "Aren't you the mailman?"

Just then, Jake stuck his head into the open space in front of Win. "Mr. Mailman! Didn't your momma tell you? You can't come to a party when you're dirty!"

Six

"On Sundays, stay within three feet of your Bible."
Velma Lee Lewis

"Listen to this one: 'Never wear white shoes except at morning worship services during June, July, and August or at June afternoon weddings.' Can you believe this woman?"

Ruth was still tired this morning. She hadn't slept well last night as she constantly replayed scenes of the party on the inside of her eyelids. "Good thing I didn't wear my white shoes this morning then," she snapped.

"Whoa! Bad night?" Janie peered over the top of the scrapbook to take in the dark circles under her aunt's eyes.

"Sorry. Need more coffee."

"Let me get it for you," Janie jumped up and nearly ran to the coffee corner. "I do think it was a good party, don't you?" She set a large cup filled with rich black coffee before Ruth.

Ruth took a swallow. Then another. "Yes. Despite the dramatic ending. What happened with Josie, anyway? I know she left, and her helper – Gerry? – cleaned everything up, but I didn't hear where she went. Did you?"

"I think Belle and Sally took her home to examine the damage and pick up her dog from that tall hero, the mailman. Then they were going to put her and her dog up with them. I imagine the house smelled too bad to sleep in. It probably needs to air out for a while, and it was too hot last night to sleep without air conditioning."

"Yeah, you're probably right. Josie said she was going to take a trip over into Arkansas. Might be a good time for her to go while her house is being repaired."

Janie mumbled, "Yep," just before breaking into loud guffaws. "Listen: 'A sitting man's knees should not spread wider than eleven inches.' Eleven! Where the hell did she come up with this stuff?"

She flipped a page of the scrapbook. "Look, Ruth." She turned the book to face Ruth and pushed it in front of her, pointing at a photo strip.

"That little character!" Ruth smiled at the four photos of Jake making grotesque faces for the camera. "I'm surprised he stuck it in the book."

"I don't think he did." She pointed to the writing next to the strip.

Ruth leaned closer, "Hmm, 'Alien replacement for four-year-old boy.' Bradley, I suppose."

"I'd guess so. Cute kid."

"Did you notice how he jumped on the potential job of clean-up for Josie? He told her he was available today to clean, move, or help however he could. Industrious."

Janie mused, "Maybe he'd like to do some work around here. Mow the grass, get rid of the unpacked boxes, clean the crap out of the shed in the back so we can use it. Probably some other stuff."

"I bet he would. But let's let him help out Josie first. Our chores will wait a bit."

"Yeah," Janie sighed. "They always do."

Ruth took the book from Janie and amused herself for several minutes looking at the photo strips and reading the sayin's. Several chuckles and snorts were eventually followed by a loud burst of laughter. "Oh, my. That woman was amazing. 'It is best to serve only white food at tea parties to prevent stains to your guests' clothing.' Lord! Can you imagine those boring parties with only white cake, milk, and sugar cookies?"

Janie held an imaginary menu in her hand and read from it dramatically: "Mayonnaise on white bread. White cheese and macaroni. White meat from the turkey and chicken with white gravy, white corn, and blancmange." By the end of the list, she nearly had to shout to be heard above Ruth's snorts of hilarity.

Janie pulled herself together to ask, "Do you think we ought to have a garden party after it cools off? We could make sure that nice mailman got his invitation this time."

"I saw you looking him over. Good looking on top of kind and helpful." Ruth winked with an exaggerated gesture.

"Oh, Ruth. Nonsense. I won't even discuss it. How tall is he, do you think? Wasn't it lucky he was home? Did you see how kind he was to Josie, er, Bea?"

"Oo-oo! I hear interest in those questions." Ruth continued in a sing-song voice, "Maybe we should invite the big, strong hero over for dinner."

"Give it up, Ruth. Now." Janie's fists found her hips.

"Let's see. Maybe I can come up with a sayin' for you. 'If a woman wants a man to notice her, she should send her aunt to invite him to dinner.' Not bad, huh?"

"Very funny. Now let it go."

Jake slid into the kitchen on stocking feet. "But I don't have it. I don't even know where it is."

Janie's frown of misunderstanding looked like disapproval to Jake, who danced from foot to foot as she asked sharply, "What are you talking about?"

"I don't know. Um, nothin'. But I don't have it. Honest."

Janie said, "Come here, you," as she ruffled his hair and kissed him on the top of his head. "OK, buster. Just see that you don't." He rubbed off her kiss before racing out of the room.

Ruth stood. "I'd better go see what he's up to. Seems to have a guilty conscience."

"Oooh, yeaaah!" Janie intoned with a giant nod of agreement.

"God, BB! What time is it? What are you doing up? Turn out that damned light." Hal King pulled a pillow over his eyes as he rolled over on the couch.

"Hal? Why are you on the couch?" Bradley rubbed fingertips across his forehead. "I didn't even know you were in town. When did you get here?"

Hal groaned and pulled the pillow tighter over his head. Bradley poured himself a cup of coffee and sat at the table where he grabbed a banana from the large bowl in front of him. He planned his strategy as he peeled the banana. He'd go to Bea Murphy's house and see how he could help. He could work today and tomorrow if she needed it. He smiled in satisfaction. There were many ways to make money if you just kept your eyes open.

He looked at Hal as he walked out the back door. Hal would never be able to get ahead on his own. His eyes were closed when he was awake!

His mother's car was missing from the driveway. She must have gone to early church service. He didn't dare take Hal's old Honda Civic clunker. For one thing, Hal would kill him. For another, the car probably wouldn't make it the couple of miles to Bea's. He walked wearily to his bicycle. God, he wanted a car. He needed three hundred more dollars for school before he could start saving up for his car. Maybe this fire would be a windfall for him.

Even at seven-thirty in the morning, riding a bicycle was too hot. By the time he arrived at Bea's, his shirt was stuck to his back and his hair was wet with sweat. He hoped at least some of the work here was inside. Outside Oklahoma in July was brutal.

Nobody was around, so he opened the back door and went into the stinking kitchen. The burnt towel was still lying on the countertop. The walls and ceiling had been blackened with smoke, and water stood in puddles on the tile floor. All the windows were open, but the smell was very strong. It needed a big exhaust fan to suck out all the bad air. There was one in the garage at his house, but he'd never be able to get it there on his bicycle. Another grating reminder of how much he needed a car.

He thought about carrying out the table and chairs. Maybe a good airing would make them usable. But he didn't know if she needed the insurance adjuster to look at the damage before it was cleared out and cleaned up. As he indecisively studied the mess, he heard a dog bark. Thinking it must be Bea's dog, he walked outside to meet her.

There was a dog coming down the sidewalk, but it was trailed by Gerry Krane instead of Bea. "Hey, Bradley. What are you doing over here so early?"

"Hey, Gerry. Who's your friend?" Bradley petted and nonsense-talked to the dog.

"That's Jessie. She's mine. But you didn't answer me. What are you doing over here so early?"

Bradley grimaced. "I wanted to try to get some work helping Miss Bea clean up this place. I guess I'm a little too quick on the draw."

Gerry grinned, "Oh, I don't know. I think it shows initiative. Bea will like that. I'm sure she'll hire you to help."

"Really? You think so?" Bradley's eagerness made Gerry smile wider.

"Count on it," she replied. "Look, here comes Bea now. Go charm her."

Bradley hurried to the street to open the car door for Bea. Gerry watched in amusement. Bradley seemed to have only one speed: fast. He made all the other kids his age look like slackers. He always had a job; always had money; always had plans. He'd do fine in this life, she thought.

Too bad his older brother, Hal, seemed totally devoid of Bradley's ambition. He was so bright and so good-looking, but there was no way she'd want to get involved again with Henry V King – King Henry V during roll calls. His mother, a Shakespeare nut, found that amusing although nobody else seemed to. She also was the only one who called her eldest son, Prince Hal. His friends just called him Hal or Prince.

When Bradley next hurried past, Gerry stopped him with a question, "Hey, Bradley, where's Prince now?"

"I don't know. He was asleep on the couch when I left."

Gerry did a double-take. "Prince's in town? Now?"

Bradley looked at her in surprise, "Well, yeah. Isn't that why you asked?"

Gerry made "uh-huh" noises as her mind ran in circles. Damn. The Prince was back in town.

Bea, Belle, and Sally walked through the house discussing what needed to be done to make it habitable again. "You can't live here, Bea," Sally said sadly. "The smell will make you sick. Why don't you gather up whatever you need for a few days and bring it to our place? You'll probably need to wash any clothes you want to wear. Seems like the smoke has gotten everywhere. Then tomorrow you can meet with Seth. He's a good builder and an honest one. But he'll be at church all day today."

"Right. I wish I could do something today. I feel helpless." Bea wandered from room to room sighing.

Bradley saw an opening, "Miss Bea, I could start moving everything out of the kitchen, wash them in a tub in the back yard, then store them in the garage. That way, they'll be ready when your kitchen is repaired. And I could hook up a big exhaust fan to clear out the smell. If you want me to." He smiled winningly at her.

"That would be helpful, Bradley. I don't have a fan though. Do you, Sal?"

"We have several. Bradley, can you get the large fan from the storeroom behind the office and bring it out?" Sally was surprised to see Bradley looking uncertain. "What's wrong?"

"I don't have a vehicle except my bicycle." Bradley muttered.

Belle grabbed his arm and led him toward her car. "Come on, we'll go get the panel truck. You can use it to bring the fan and a big washtub back with you." As she got into the car, she hollered back to Sally and Bea, "We'll be back shortly. You want anything else?"

Sally said, "Coffee," but Belle ignored her with a wave of her hand before she drove off.

"How much do you think I should pay Bradley for his help?" Bea asked.

"Ask him. He's an honest worker. And your insurance should cover your expenses. Have you called your agent?"

"Yeah. He said he'd be here tomorrow at 8:00 with an ad-juster." She walked back into the kitchen and stared at the burned cloth on the counter. "I can't figure out how that towel got against the burner. I know I didn't have a towel by the stove. I never do."

Sally frowned, "Doesn't really matter, does it? Spilt milk."

"I guess you're right." She found a stack of grocery bags and carried them into her bedroom where she began pulling out clothes and shoes and stuffing them into bags.

"Can I help?" Sally offered, standing in the doorway to the bathroom. "Want me to open windows or something?"

"No, thanks, Sal. I'll get Bradley to do that. I just want to get some things out of here and get them cleaned up so I can use them." She took a bag into the bathroom and stuffed cosmetics and medicine bottles into it. "I guess I'll have to delay my trip. And I don't know what I'll do about Gerry."

"What about Gerry? Isn't she going to keep working for you?"

"Well, yes, but only for a while. The plan was she'd learn the ropes and take over while I went to Arkansas. Then she'd be off on another job when I got back. I can't really afford to hire her for very long." Bea had filled six bags and began to carry them outside.

"After you get Seth going on renovating, will you really need to be here? Maybe it would be a good time for you to be gone." Sally picked up one bag, all she could carry since her cane took one hand.

Bea's energy flagged as she reached the porch. She flopped in-to a wicker chair, strewing grocery bags around her feet. "Maybe you're right. Maybe I should just go. Lord, I don't know what to do."

"Luckily, you don't have to decide today." Sally gave Bea's shoulder a squeeze as she walked past her on the way to the oth-er chair. "I sure hope Belle brings some coffee."

Just then, Belle's car and the kennel's panel truck turned into the driveway. Belle brought a picnic basket onto the porch. "I thought you ought to take a little break," she said as she got out cups, napkins, a thermos of coffee, and a bag of donuts. "Feed a problem. Isn't that what your Gran always said, Sally?"

Sally's face softened, "Yep. She had her sayin's too." She chuckled, "That was fun at the party last night, remembering Velma Lee's edicts. I wonder where Janie got the idea to do that?"

Bea said softly, "I gave it to her. We were talking about why everyone was late to the party, and I told her about Miss Velma Lee."

"Oh, yeah. The fifteen minute rule. I'm so used to it by now that it doesn't even seem strange any more." Belle pursed her lips. "I wonder what other sayin's have turned into custom?" She looked around the porch at the bags Bea had packed. Sticking out of the top of one was a Bible. Belle pointed at it and grinned, "Isn't that a little more than three feet away from you, Bea?"

Seven

"Never compliment anyone after dark."
Velma Lee Lewis

"So Bea got Seth working on the restoration, left Shep with Belle and Sally, and took off for Arkansas. I think she'll be gone two or three weeks." Gerry poured another cup of coffee for Ruth and Janie who had come into the diner for the first time. Jake was under the table racing two small cars around chair legs and across napkin and silverware obstacles.

"I wonder if she went back to Conway," Ruth speculated. "If she hasn't been there in a while, she won't know it. It's grown so much since we were in school there."

"You went to school with Bea in Conway, Arkansas? I didn't know she was from Arkansas. I thought she was from over around Tahlequah." Gerry stacked dirty dishes and the coffee pot onto her tray.

"I just know she was in school with me from about the seventh grade onward." Ruth ducked under the table. "Jake, get your stuff and come up here now. We're about ready to leave."

Jake's curly head popped up beside his mother. "Are we going home now?"

Janie lay her hand on his head, "Soon, bud. Climb up in your chair and drink the rest of your milk."

"Aww, Momma."

Janie's stern look quieted Jake's moan although it did not hasten his obedience. "Now, Jake," she said quietly.

Jake looked at her to judge her seriousness, then climbed into his chair and lifted his glass.

"How are you doing with the diner while Josie, er, Bea's away? I understand you've only worked here a short time." Ruth inquired while keeping a weather eye on Jake.

"That's right. I'm just filling in for her for a few weeks. It gave me a job when I needed it and gave her a break."

"Do you have any leads for another job?" Janie asked.

"I've been working on a writing project. I need to get a little further along and then see if I can sell it. I had gotten stuck and nearly gave up, but I've been writing again lately. I think it might work out."

"Boy, I understand. I've got a contract to illustrate a children's book, and I hit a wall for a while. I'm afraid to even say so, but I think I'm past it. At least I've left more lines than I've erased lately."

Gerry's wide smile crinkled the skin at the corner of her eyes. "Hey, maybe we should start a group, The Unstuck Club, or something."

"Erasers Anonymous?" Janie contributed.

"I like it. EA. Maybe we should have a meeting."

"Good idea. How about at my house tomorrow night after you close the diner. We'll kill a bottle of wine and tell stories about stoppered creativity."

"Thanks. I'll be there. About nine, okay?" Gerry carried away the detritus of breakfast as Janie and Ruth steered Jake out the door.

At nine o'clock the next evening Gerry was dancing through puddles on her way to Janie's house. The afternoon thundershower had dropped about an inch of rain and lowered the temperature by fifteen degrees. It was still steamy, but it felt like softer heat now. A steam bath rather than a sauna.

Janie was sitting on the porch nursing a tall frosty glass. "Hey, I'm glad you came over. I'm drinking a spritzer of Sauvignon Blanc and lime. Want one?"

Gerry closed the screened door and wiped her wet feet on a well-placed mat. "Sounds wonderful." She set the basket she'd brought with her on a low table in front of an empty rocker. "I brought some munchies." She pulled out a bowl of mixed nuts and another of some sort of small cracker.

"What are those?" Janie asked as she went inside for Gerry's drink.

"Sesame Stix," Gerry called after her. "My downfall." She took a handful and began to pop them into her mouth as she dropped into the rocker next to the large wicker chair that Janie had inhabited.

Janie returned with a glass, a bottle of wine, a bottle of seltzer, a sliced lime, and an ice bucket arranged on a wicker tray. "Now we should be set."

Gerry stopped Janie from sitting, "Before we settle in, could I see some of your paintings?"

Janie looked startled, but recovered to say graciously, "Sure. Come on in." She led the way to the back of the house where she opened a door into a large, partially finished room. "It's missing most of the wallboard and has never been painted, but it's perfect for me to use as a studio. And it's far enough from Jake's room and his playroom-cum-dining room that I don't hear his noise." She opened a large portfolio lying on a table. "Here are the most recent paintings I've been working on." She pulled out two stiff-backed paintings and laid them on the table.

Gerry's eyes widened, "Wow! These are really cool." She stood back to look at the paintings together, then moved close to examine the details. "I'm knocked out. I was expecting some sort of kiddie drawings." She touched a large swirl of yellows and oranges that covered nearly two-thirds of one of the pieces. "Fire?"

Janie's eyebrow popped up as a half-smile touched her lips. "Very good. You got it in one."

Gerry gestured toward the portfolio, "May I look at the others?" At Janie's nod, she pulled out ten more paintings, lining them up, one by one, on the table. "Wow! These are wonderful. Not what I expected. When Ruth told me about your Wee Folk, I envisioned elves and fairies. But these look more like small homeless people."

"Yes!" Janie pumped her fist in the air. "You're the first one to get it immediately. The book these illustrate is about differences among people. And how those who don't fit in form their own communities."

Gerry nodded seriously, "And thus the homeless look. I like how you kept it from being a parody – they're not frightening or ridiculous."

"Wow! Can I pay you to come over and praise me when I'm feeling uncertain?"

"Sure. But really, I think they're very good. The people look stoic and, oh, I don't know, charmingly noble."

"OK. You've earned a bonus before you've even started working as my official praiser." Janie's grin grew even wider.

"Yeah, I could use a praiser, too." Gerry looked wistfully at the paintings. "You're lucky that your work can be accessed so readily. You can get an instant reaction – positive or negative. Mine takes longer to evaluate."

"I hadn't thought of that. It's not much of a hardship for you to look at my paintings. You can do it in under five minutes. But reading your stories is a commitment of time and attention."

"Exactly. Thus, nobody else has seen my work. And no praise, no critique, nada. I'm on my own." Gerry felt herself about to slip into a pity party. "Oh, damn. I didn't mean to whine. Let's go back out on the porch and drink."

"OK. Sure." Janie lagged behind, quietly closing the door of her studio after a last look around. "Yes!" she whispered before following Gerry outside.

"So what are you writing? I'd be happy to read it if you want," Janie offered as she added ice to her drink.

"I've been working on a group of stories about Sally O'Neill, Belle Sheppard, and BellWhether Kennels. I worked at the kennel when I was in high school. I loved listening to their stories of their early days when they were just getting started with dogs.

"I made notes and tried to write some of their stories back then, but got nowhere. I found those notebooks when I packed to move back here. I thought maybe I could do better now."

"So how much have you written?"

"Three chapters. Sally's first dog. Belle's first dog. And the first dog they bred."

"Have you shown it to them?" Janie grabbed another handful of Sesame Stix. "These are really good."

"Told you." Gerry sighed. "No, I haven't shown it to anyone. I'd hoped to interest them in funding me while I write it and get it published, then promote its sale. But I haven't felt certain enough about it to show them." She shrugged. "As I said – no feedback."

"Let me read it. I'm a pretty good critic."

Gerry looked at her, appraising her seriousness. "OK. I need to finish the fourth chapter, the one about Sally's first bloodhound. That should be enough to give a good flavor for what I'm trying to do. But you can read what I have. It's about thirty pages."

"Go get it. I'll read it tonight."

"Really?"

"Yes, then come over tomorrow night after you get off work, praise my work some more, and I'll tell you what I think."

Gerry stood but looked hard at Janie. "You're serious?"

Janie brushed the air in front of her with both hands. "Go. And bring some more of those sesame things if you have any." She grabbed another handful as she spoke.

Gerry practically ran back to her house, gathered her first three chapters into a folder, grabbed the bag of Sesame Stix, and dashed out again, nearly colliding with Win.

"Whoa, Nelly! Where are you dashing off to?" Win grabbed her by the upper arms to steady her.

"Oh. Sorry, Smoke. I'm going back to Janie's. I just came home for reinforcements." She held up the bag of Sesame Stix. As she did, she saw another figure in the shadows behind Win. "Somebody with you?"

"Hey, Ger," said a deep voice. Then Hal King stepped into the light. "I ran into Smoke at Benney's. He invited me over for another beer. Said you lived around here. We came with a peace offering." He held up a six-pack.

"Prince! Damn. I heard you were in town. Saw Bradley yesterday." She allowed herself to be pulled into a hug but held herself stiffly back. She would not allow herself to melt against him. Even so, he felt good. "Why a peace offering? We're not at war."

He chuckled, "No. Not war. I just thought you might be pissed that I never called you."

Gerry sucked in a breath and held it for a count of ten then slowly exhaled. "You don't owe me anything." He was even better looking than the last time she saw him. Five years ago. "Janie and I are having a drink on her porch. Come on over. Meet our new neighbor."

Hal and Win exchanged glances then shrugged. "Why not?" Win turned toward the street. "But I've met her."

"Oh, yeah. When you blew off her party." Gerry paused a moment, "On second thought, you better go home. She won't want you rude thing coming over tonight."

"I thought I explained that," Win began.

Gerry cut him off, "I'm just messing with you. It'll be fine. Come on."

As they arrived at the steps to Janie's porch, she greeted them from inside. "Boy, I need to be careful. I sent you home for treats and look what you brought back."

Gerry felt the blood rise in her face. It was hard being a red-head prone to blushing. She'd been teased about it her entire life. Once she calmed down, she introduced Janie and Hal. Then she said, "Janie, I think you've met Smoke, er, Win Reynolds."

Win put out his hand and said formally, "Miss Stewart."

Janie shook his hand, holding it a bit longer than necessary. "I've met you three times now. I think you can dispense with the 'Miss Stewart' and just call me Janie."

Win nodded, "Janie. Thank you for letting us crash your party."

"Seems fair since you skipped my last one." She winked at him as she poured Gerry's Sesame Stix into a bowl and handed it around.

Hal took one and ate it dramatically. "Still get these at Bristow's?"

Gerry nodded.

"What's Bristow's?" Janie asked. "I need to know about the place that makes these."

Gerry grinned as she slapped herself on the butt, "You sure?"

Win offered, "I'll take you there. It's kind of hard to find the first time. But it's an interesting drive. And your boy would like the petting zoo."

Janie handed the bowl to Win. "Thank you. I'd like that. And I'm sure Jake will."

"How about Saturday afternoon. I'm off Saturday."

"Unless you have to dodge another party or put out another fire," Gerry gibed.

The next morning Janie sat at the kitchen table flipping through Gerry's stories again. She had stayed up late reading them, and she liked them. She'd met Belle and Sally a couple of times and could hear their voices telling the stories. Gerry had done that well. She pulled at her bottom lip as she drank her morning smoothie. She wouldn't have to lie when she praised Gerry's work. Thank God.

"Morning, Ruth," she greeted her aunt as Ruth came into the kitchen from the back porch.

"Hey, sleepyhead. Jake and I've been up for hours. He's out back deciding on where to build the fort."

"A fort? How's this fort going to be built?"

"I think he plans to be the boss and recruit some labor. Maybe the mailman."

"He stopped by last night. With Gerry and a guy named Hal. Or Prince."

Ruth wagged her eyebrows.

"And before you start, he's invited me and Jake to go to Bristow's, whatever that is, on Saturday afternoon."

"Ahh."

"Don't start."

"I didn't say anything."

"You didn't have to. I can read your mind."

Ruth placed her middle finger across her forehead. "Then read this."

Janie chuckled, "You are bad!"

Ruth shrugged coyly and batted her eyes.

"Hey, before I forget, I've got something I want you to read. Gerry brought me the first three chapters of a piece she's writing. I read it, but I'd like your opinion, too, before I tell her what I think."

"That bad?"

"No. Just the opposite. I think it's very good. See what you think if you have time. She's coming over tonight for my reaction." Janie handed the folder to Ruth.

Ruth flipped through its contents. "OK. I'll have my secretary cancel all my afternoon appointments." She carried the folder to her chair in the den and settled in to read.

About an hour later, Ruth went looking for Janie. She found her in the back yard with Jake, staking off a corner of the yard.

"I read Gerry's stories," Ruth announced as she stepped inside the future fort.

"And?"

"And I agree with you. I think they're quite good. For the little I know of Belle and Sally, I think she's got their voices just right."

"I thought so, too. Thanks. I'll tell her you agree with me. Maybe that will encourage her to write some more."

"Has she shown it to Belle and Sally?"

"No. But she said she will as soon as she finishes another chapter. She hopes to get them to fund her while she finishes writing it and getting it published."

"They should. It would be great advertising for their kennel." She turned back to the house, announcing over her shoulder, "Your corners aren't square."

"What's that mean, Momma? Our corners aren't square?" Jake peered at the spot in front of him where Janie had driven a stake.

"It means we need to measure better. Can you hold this stick straight and don't let it move?"

Jake planted his feet and squinted his eyes, "I promise I won't let it move." He held the stake between his feet and tilted toward his chin. There was no way to accurately measure from the stick held at that angle. "Who needs square corners anyway?" Janie hollered at the door Ruth had just closed behind her.

Gerry showed up at Janie's house a few minutes after nine that night. She'd been jittery all day, afraid of what Janie would tell her.

When Janie saw her climb the steps, she yelled, "It's good. It's really good!"

Gerry grinned and came inside. Janie sat in the same chair she'd occupied the previous night.

"I didn't want you to be nervous about asking me what I thought," Janie said, lifting her glass in salute. "Here's to a great start to your writing career!"

"Here, here!" Ruth added from the corner. "I read it, too, Gerry. And I agree. You've got a great beginning. You caught Belle and Sally exactly."

Gerry looked back and forth between them, "Really? You really think so?"

They nodded in unison.

"Whew!" Gerry blew her breath out in a whoosh. "I've stewed about it all day."

"Stew no more!" Ruth commanded. "Finish your next chapter and show it to Belle and Sally." She stood to go inside. "Ruth has spoken." Only a slight wobble at the end of her walk across the porch gave away the two glasses of wine she'd drunk.

"Thanks, Ruth!" Gerry said earnestly.

Ruth waved backward over her shoulder as she went inside. "Let me read the rest of it when you're done. I'm interested in what happens."

Gerry glowed.

Janie inquired, "So you want me as your praise-meister?"

Gerry impulsively reached across the table and squeezed Janie's hand. "Thank you! Thank you! I think I'll go home now and finish the next chapter." She picked up her folder, bowed toward Janie, and dashed off the porch and down the walk.

"Yep, you need me as your praise-meister," she said softly to a disappearing back.

Eight

"Pray in your bedrooms, not on the street."
Velma Lee Lewis

The next morning, Gerry called BellWhether Kennels as soon as the morning rush of ranchers eating breakfast had died down. Sally answered the phone almost before it rang. "Hi, Sally, it's Gerry Krane. Were you sitting on top of the phone?"

Sally laughed, "No. I had just reached for it to make a call. When it rang, I jerked back like it had fangs. Surprised I didn't drop it. So, what can I do for you, Gerry? Have you heard from Bea?"

"No. I haven't heard from her yet. I hope she's having a good trip. What I wanted was to ask if I could come talk with you and Belle tomorrow afternoon. I'd like to show you a project I'm working on."

"That's fine with me. I'll have to check with Belle. I can let you know."

"That's good. Would two o'clock be all right?"

"Sure. But why are you being so mysterious? Can't you just tell me?"

Gerry's nerves were about to get the best of her. She only wanted to get off the phone quickly. "It's not a mystery. I just have to show you some things. I'll tell you everything tomorrow. See you then." She hung up and dashed for the bathroom. She had always had a nervous stomach.

After her stomach settled, she admitted she was proud of herself. She was pleased with the progress she'd made by writing until nearly three o'clock that morning. She'd finished the chapter about Sally's first bloodhound, and she'd arranged to show her work to Sally and Belle.

BellWhether Tails

Nosy – 1974

In July, the sheriff wrangled a donation from a wealthy rancher to add a mantrailing dog to his K-9 corps. He sent Sally to South Georgia to check out a bloodhound kennel and training school. She says because nobody else wanted to go to the swamps in July.

When she came back from Georgia with a bloodhound pup, I thought she'd lost her mind. "Bloodhounds don't herd," I had reminded her.

She looked at me in exasperation, "No, they track." She held the gangly black and tan bundle. She played with its ears and the loose skin on its face and neck. "You've pretty well taken over the herding and the breeding of the border collies," she said mildly.

"I'm sorry. I didn't mean to shove you aside."

Sally shook her head. "No. That's not what I meant. It's just that you're so much better at it. Look at all the winning you've done with Dillon and the others. You've established a name for yourself. I only ever did it for fun."

"I do it for fun, too," I objected.

"Oh, I know. But you're in it to win. I'm in it to play with my dog." She smiled wryly. "You're more serious. More competitive."

"Hmm. Maybe. Are you going to be serious with a bloodhound?" I looked doubtful, I know.

"I wish you could have gone to Georgia with me. Then you'd understand better." She took a breath, "Unless you make a living from the livestock you herd, you're just playing. But when you're tracking a lost child, that's not play. It's serious. Life or death serious." She looked hopefully at me. "I'm not explaining myself very well."

"No."

"OK. I'll try a different way." She paused, then continued quickly, "I'm in law enforcement. I see how much help a good mantrailer will be for the department. I want to be the handler, the trainer, the go-to person for the dog the sheriff's department is getting. And I want to train another dog, to see if I can. Then, we'll see." Her eyes pleaded for understanding.

"So you bought this puppy." I smoothed my hand across her soft ears. "Isn't it more normal to buy a trained dog?"

"Yes. And we're going to get a trained one for the department. But I want to train one for myself. Jo Beth said she'd help train me. She's really amazing. You should see her."

"Won't that mean more trips to Georgia?"

"Yes. But I really want to try this. The feeling I got working with a dog on the scent is unlike anything else. Because of the *seriousness* of it. I want to repeat that. I want to be useful."

I thought I understood. Sally had lost both her Gran and Gramps within three months of each other. She'd pulled away from the dogs and the ranch.

"Where will you keep the pup?" Her place in town had too small a yard for an active pup.

"I thought I'd move to the ranch. Sell the house in town."

"Really?" I was flabbergasted. I hadn't seen that coming.

Sally nodded slowly. "I thought about it all the way home from Georgia. I thought we could build a real kennel. You'd have a better place for the collies and I'd have a place for the bloodhounds. You could move out there, too. Hell, you practically live there now."

That was true. With my dogs and sheep and cattle at the ranch, I spent very little time in my house in town. "You suggesting we share the house?"

"Yep. There's plenty of room. And I think you should buy a couple of really good dogs to breed with our pack. You haven't had pups in over four years since Miss Kitty got too old. If you want to keep this line alive, you've got to bring in fresh blood."

"I know. I've been looking at a kennel in Scotland. They've got top-notch dogs to complement our line. I think a couple of bitches to breed to our boys – Chester for one has qualities I don't want to lose."

"Do you want to keep trialing?" Sally cocked her head to watch my reaction.

I looked at her with a nod. "Yeah. I do."

"Then let's do it!"

I picked up the puppy and held her out in front of me. "First, I have an important question. What's her name?"

Sally ran her hand down the pup's back. "Nosy." She smiled, "Her name's Nosy."

By late October our plans were underway. Sally had sold her house and moved to the ranch. I was set to move on Halloween. The kennel building was in the dry with seven runs complete.

Sally caught me as I walked into the office on the Monday before Halloween. "Bell, we need to talk. Something's come up."

I fell into step beside her. "What?"

"Jo Beth called. She had a cancellation and has a dog ready for its first training session with its new handler. The sheriff's getting eager for his dog. I have to go to Georgia on Saturday."

"Oh." My mind raced. How could I manage all the dogs and moving with Sally gone?

"I'm sorry. I tried to postpone for a couple weeks but it won't work for Jo Beth."

"Oh." I knew I wasn't giving her much but I didn't have much to give just then. Maybe I could hire some help. But who?

"Bell, you okay?" Sally wrinkled her forehead in concern.

"Who's that kid that's always coming around looking for work? J.D.'s grandson?"

Sally's eyebrows pulled closer together then relaxed, "Oh. Hire some help?" She took a deep breath, "I don't know – Jimmy or Johnny. No. Doug."

"Yeah, Doug. Whose is he?"

"Doyle's, I think. Want me to call?"

"Yeah. See if he's free on Saturday and Sunday."

And so I hired my first helper. Doug McAllister. Eighteen years old, hard worker, dog lover.

Sally came home without a dog. "The dog slated for us, Marlene, started limping badly a couple days ago. Jo Beth wouldn't let me bring her back until she's checked out and recovered. She didn't charge the department for the class."

"The sheriff should be OK with that, then." I put in. I knew his budget was tight.

"He's still out for my time and expenses if Marlene doesn't improve and I have to do this again with another dog. But I learned so much, maybe I can convince the sheriff it was worth it. And I can't wait to start teaching Nosy what I learned."

By this time, I was settled at the ranch. Doug was working three afternoons a week. He helped with the dogs, the kennel, and other chores around the farm.

Sally threw all her energy into training Nosy. Her long-distance conversations with Jo Beth left her energized and excited. Nosy, she told me, was the result of good breeding and natural talent. It was up to her to guide Nosy to be the best mantrailer in Kansas.

"Trailing and tracking are two different things," Sally told me and anyone else who would listen. You'd think she'd created bloodhounds the way she carried on. "All dogs can learn to track, and some can learn to trail, but bloodhounds are born to trail."

According to Jo Beth, whom Sally quoted endlessly, tracking is the ability to follow human scent; trailing is the ability to distinguish and follow a specific person's scent and identify that person. A tracking dog follows footsteps and clues; a trailing dog follows body scent. Jo Beth believed in teaching her bloodhounds to track first, then "letting them become bloodhounds" and trail. Tracking can be a useful tool for a good trailer, she said.

Anyway, Sally trained Nosy to track. She laid tracks, dropping food as rewards and objects as clues. She spent hours with Nosy every day. Her conversations were filled with new terms like "skin rafts" and "scent waves." She was happy.

The only irritant in her life was the sheriff. Jo Beth decided that Marlene wouldn't recover enough to be a working dog. Sally and the sheriff had to wait for the next group of dogs, about three months, and he was not happy about it.

I had started corresponding with Emma MacLeod of Skye Collies in Dunvegan, Isle of Skye, Scotland. I wanted to buy two of her female pups – the planned foundation bitches of my breeding program. She had two litters on the ground with three nice bitches in one and two in the other. She wanted time for them to grow into their abilities before selling me one from each litter. She said she had to see which "wee lasses" she would keep and which two she'd send to me.

Right after Christmas, I got the letter. My two girls, Hope and Grace, were booked on a flight to Kansas City on January 6. I wanted to make sure I got there on time, so I planned to leave Dodge City on the fourth and return on the seventh. That gave me a day's leeway for problems, breakdowns, or emergencies. Doug would do extra duty to help Sally out while I was gone. He'd do all the feeding and exercising of the dogs. She was nearly as excited as I was.

My biggest concern was the weather. A blizzard could blow up in January with little warning. I fitted out my van with emergency supplies and headed out early on the morning of January 4, 1975. I made the drive without mishap and found a motel just west of the city where I spent my just-in-case day doing a bit of sightseeing and reading. On the morning of the sixth, I drove to the new airport that seemed about halfway from the city to the Iowa border, and collected my new dogs.

These girls were slighter than my other dogs and had wispier coats. Both stared at me intently as I spoke to them in a soft, reassuring voice. Grace was a beautifully marked black and white. Her symmetrical face was topped with perfectly tipped ears. Hope, on the other hand, looked slightly moldy – her blue merle markings were blotchy and uneven. One ear pricked while the other flopped. Her left eye was surrounded by a dark patch, but her right eye had only a touch of black at the outer corner. I figured Emma had named them right and I could only hope that these frightened girls were worth the expense and effort.

I crated them in the back of the van and drove through the city. I wondered where my relatives lived but made no attempt to contact them. They were no part of my life.

I got home just before dark on the sixth, beating a big storm by only a few hours.

Sally was in a tizzy when I arrived. Someone had been walking around outside the kennel at night, stirring up the dogs.

I listened to her as I got Hope and Grace situated in their new quarters and said hello to the others. Sally talked fast, as she did when she was upset, "I saw footprints leading from the edge of the woods to the kennel building. Big prints – too big for me or Doug. And the dogs all went crazy barking both nights you were gone. Wee hours barking." She gestured wildly, slapping her hand against the gate of Hope's run.

"Did you follow the tracks?" I asked mildly, trying to tone down her excitement level.

"Only to the edge of the woods. Then they disappeared in the undergrowth."

I looked at her in astonishment, "Don't you have a bloodhound?"

She clapped a hand over her mouth. "I forgot."

"You forgot?" I couldn't prevent my voice from rising in incredulity. "How could you forget?"

Sally sadly shook her head from side to side. "I felt violated. Remember when you were first training Dillon and we had that peeping tom? I felt like that. I guess I thought I couldn't do anything this time since we never found out anything last time. And we couldn't find out who knocked Gramps off his tractor either."

I looked at her grimly, "We acted like victims then. We don't have to now. Go get Nosy."

"Now? She's not fully trained. And aren't you tired after your drive?"

"It's going to snow. I know Nosy's inexperienced so why make it harder on her. Let's see if she can pick up the trail."

I stood aside to let Sally get Nosy out of her kennel, into her tracking harness, and to the area where the footprints were clearest. She knelt beside Nosy, whispered in her ear. Then Sally stood up and issued her command, "Go Find."

Nosy sniffed the footprints and raised her head to look to her left. She took a few steps, corrected her heading, then took off for the edge of the woods. And into them. Sally followed, holding the thirty-foot lead. She told me to follow along behind her.

After what seemed like an hour, we burst out of the woods at the edge of a field. A path wound from us, around an outbuilding, and toward a house at the top of the hill. J.D.'s house. Nosy bayed loudly. Sally pounded her sides, told her what a good dog she was. Then she looked a question at me.

"I don't know," I told her. "I don't know what we do now."

Sally rose after removing Nosy's harness and brushed the first snowflakes from her back. "Why would he start bothering us again? It was years ago."

I shrugged. "Maybe he's feeling safe again."

"Then let's make him feel un-safe." Sally stomped the ground dramatically. "Let's make him feel damned un-safe."

The kennel building was a thirty-two foot square surrounded by a six-foot tall chain link fence placed twelve feet from the building. That created a forty-four foot enclosed area. On each side of the building were five runs, each four feet wide and six feet long inside the building and twelve feet long outside. A flap-door in the wall provided access in and out. A gate on the end inside let us into the run. In the corners where the interior runs met, we installed a diagonal gate, creating a nearly six-foot square space for puppies or breeding pairs. These corner runs opened onto twelve by twelve yards where multiple dogs could run together.

Two of the runs, one on the east and one on the north, lacked end-gates inside, end fence outside, and substituted a people-sized door for a flap-door. These were the passageways into the building.

The center of the building was open – a twenty-foot square that held two desks, three chairs, food bins, and storage cabinets. High windows in each wall provided light and ventilation. We supplemented that with a large exhaust fan in the south wall and central heat and air throughout. Each run had a drain in its concrete floor for easy clean-up. We hoped we'd thought of everything.

We hadn't. We forgot outside lighting. After the brush with the midnight visitor, we installed large flood lights on poles at every corner of the yard. We hooked out-facing motion detectors to the floods. Any movement outside the fence caused the floods to switch on, lighting about a hundred feet completely around the building.

The first night we had the lights working, Sally and I stayed in the kennel building after dark, waiting. We had kept Doug out of it, unsure if his family was involved. We turned on only the night light that was always on. Then we waited. Sal was good at it. She was used to stake-outs. I wasn't. I was jittery, pacing back and forth across the open space in the center of the building.

Sally finally told me to set my butt down. "You are keeping the dogs stirred up. Now settle down or go to the house." She could be very bossy.

Around eleven o'clock, Dillon started barking, followed by the others. Within a few seconds, the lights on the south side of the yard flashed on. Sally and I ran to look out the windows. We saw the shape of a man sprint toward the tree-line. Sally ran out the east door and shot her twelve-gauge high into the treetops above the disappearing man.

For the next several nights, the spotlights came on between eleven o'clock and midnight. Then they stopped except for the intermittent visits of fox, raccoons, and once, a neighbor's loose mule.

Sally was dancing-happy. She was sure we'd taken care of our problem.

I was happy, too, as soon as I hung the black-out curtains in my bedroom. Those damned lights shone right into my eyes every time a night creature came visiting.

Gerry nodded as she read through her notebook. She thought she'd done okay with Nosy. Tomorrow she'd find out what Sally and Belle thought.

Janie flitted through her house like a crazed butterfly. "What in hell is up with you?" Ruth demanded after watching her for several moments.

"Win is picking me up at two o'clock. We're going somewhere called Bristow's, and I don't have anything to wear."

"Oh, for God's sakes, Jane Ann. How old are you? You're not going to a royal audience, and it's 110 degrees. Get a grip. Put on a t-shirt and a pair of shorts." Ruth wandered back to the kitchen for another cup of coffee, muttering as she went, "God, give me strength."

Janie stomped back to her room muttering about Ruth not understanding anything. Jake met her in the hall. "Are you having a sissy fit, Momma?" he asked, looking at her quizzically.

"A sissy fit? What do you mean, Jake?"

"Yesterday I got mad at horsie for making me fall down, and Aunt Ruthie told me not to have a sissy fit."

Janie took a deep breath. "I guess I was having a sissy fit. But you saved me." She leaned over and gave him a hug. "Want to come help me find something to wear?"

He scowled, "No! I want to work on my fort." He shook his head at her. "You said you'd help."

"I will help. Tomorrow. Today I have to get ready for our trip with Win, er, Mr. Mailman. You can play outside until lunch then you have to get a bath and put on clean clothes."

"I am clean! I tooked a bath last night. Don't need a other bath." Jake stalked off down the hall, shaking his head and muttering.

"Well, I've handled the morning well," Janie said to herself as she opened her closet. A t-shirt and shorts, huh? Ruth was probably right, dammit. And so was Jake. She had had a sissy fit.

Win arrived promptly at two o'clock driving a mini-van. "Is that your car?" Janie asked as they walked toward it. "I mean, do you own it?"

Win looked puzzled. "Yes, I own it. Why?"

"Oh, nothing. I just had you pegged as the sports car type."

"Nope. Not me. I don't fit most sports cars, and I need something with some room to haul my gardening supplies."

Janie started to walk toward her car when Win said, "Aren't you going to ride with me?"

"Sure. I'm just getting Jake's booster seat."

"Um, you don't need to. I have one." Win's sheepish expression made Janie laugh. "It came with the van. I mean, it's built in. Here, look." He opened the back door and showed her the integrated booster seat in the middle section of the seat.

Janie looked at him carefully, "You don't have kids, do you?"

"No. I got a great deal on this van, and that seat was already in it. It wasn't worth it to have it removed. Normally, I keep it folded up, like this." He flipped up the bottom of the booster seat and the entire thing disappeared inside the seatback. "I thought it would be perfect for Jake. Today. I mean. To ride in." He knew he was blathering but couldn't help himself.

Janie helped him out, "Well, hey, that's great. Look, Jake," she called. "There's a special seat just for you." Jake watched gleefully as Win pulled the seat out of its hiding spot again.

"Wowee!" Jake climbed into the seat and allowed Win to buckle him in securely. "What's that?" he asked, pointing at a small screen that slid down from the ceiling in front of him.

"That's a special surprise. Here put these on." Win handed him a set of earphones and slid them around Jake's neck. "Now, see those buttons?" He indicated two large buttons in the arm of Jake's seat. "Green is for Go, and red is for...."

"STOP!" Jake shouted.

"Right. Now push the green button." Jake pushed it and looked in amazement as "Toy Story 3" began playing on the small screen.

"Wowee!" he shouted again. "Look, Momma. Wowee!"

Win adjusted Jake's earphone volume and closed the back door. He opened the front door for Janie and said, "You look nice today. Cool and casual. Just right." He gave her a big smile as he walked around the front of the van to get into the driver's seat. He was feeling good. He thought he was starting out on the right foot for a change. "Please, God," he begged silently, "don't let me mess this up."

It would take about forty minutes for them to reach Bristow's, Win told Janie. They had a pleasant ride discussing Janie's art, Win's garden, Janie's reasons for moving to Plainview, and the death of Win's mother.

About ten minutes before they arrived, Janie saw the first "Bristow's Because" sign along the road. Then more came into view along the road, attached to buildings, and painted on barn roofs. "Like 'See Rock City', I guess," Janie mused. Win frowned and shook his head. "You don't know about Rock City?" she asked. At his second head-shake, she explained about the Chattanooga attraction that advertised all over the Southeast, paying farmers to paint their roofs.

Win thought for a minute before asking, "Is Rock City worth seeing?" When Janie nodded, he said, "Ah," and pointedly closed his mouth.

"You're not going to tell me about it, are you?"

"About what?"

"Bristow's."

"Nope. You'll just have to see it for yourself."

Janie pointedly turned away from Win and toward Jake in the backseat. He had hardly made a sound since they left home. "You okay, Jakester?" she asked loudly enough to be heard over the movie's soundtrack.

Jake glanced at her and smiled, jerked a thumb upward, then looked back to the movie.

She turned back to the front seat, catching Win's smile as she did. "You think you're pretty smart, don't you? Getting Jake that DVD?"

"I already had it. I'm just letting him watch it."

"You had it? Really?" Janie's expression showed her beginning worry about Win – a car seat, a kiddie DVD, and no kids.

"It came with the van."

"You're kidding?"

"Yes, but it was a good answer."

Janie chuckled and looked out the side window at the passing scenery – one flat field after the other, occasionally a sprinkling of cattle. Not a very exciting landscape. "So what town is Bristow's in?"

"Not in a town."

"I just can't imagine what it will be like."

"Nope. You can't."

"OK, smart guy. How's this? As we get closer, the 'Bristow's Because' signs will get closer together until they line the sides of the highway. A large yellow arrow, blinking, will point the way into a long driveway. Signs line the driveway, too. At the end of the drive is a sprawling building painted brown and yellow with 'Bristow's Because' painted on the steeply slanted roof."

"Where'd you see a photo? Did you Google it?" Win asked as his mouth twitched into a grin.

"Just wait. I'll bet I'm right." Janie sighed and leaned back against the window, studying Win. "This really was nice of you to bring us clear out here."

"I'm a nice guy," he agreed. "And I love Sesame Stix."

At last they arrived. The approach to the building was not nearly so dramatic as Janie had envisioned, but there were many "Bristow's Because" signs on the highway and around the parking lot.

There was also a painted roof, but the building was red with yellow and blue trim. Matching balloons were tied to posts everywhere – some real and some painted on plywood. Off to one side was a petting zoo that immediately caught Jake's eye.

Janie promised a visit to the zoo on their way out. First, she told Jake, they needed to see what was inside. She opened the large glass door to a blast of cold air and loud circus music. Clowns patrolled the entry lobby holding out bowls of Sesame Stix to all the visitors.

At the end of the lobby was a glass wall exposing a small factory with about a dozen workers, all dressed in bright colors. They were mixing dough, squeezing small stix out of large pastry bags onto trays, putting trays in and out of ovens, and packaging the resulting Sesame Stix in their distinctive red, blue, and yellow cellophane bags.

"Don't tell me all the Sesame Stix in the world are made right here!" Janie demanded.

Win chuckled, "No, but it makes a good show, doesn't it? The rest of this complex houses the real, fully-mechanized factory that also makes chips of various kinds, cookies, crackers, and pretzels. Sort of an Okie Nabisco."

Janie grinned at Win's description. When she looked down at Jake, her grin widened. He was mesmerized. He poked one Sesame Stix bit after another into his mouth as his eyes followed the factory workers skipping between work areas. Janie had to shake his shoulder to get his attention.

"Hey, bud, you want to get something to drink? I thought I saw a soda fountain at the other end of the room." Jake nodded, continuing to eat Sesame Stix at a steady pace. Janie turned to Win, "Do these things have some sort of psychotropic drugs in them?"

"You'd think so, wouldn't you. Let's fight drugs with drugs. Jazz him up a little with a hit of caffeine in a Diet Cola. Then take him out to run with the animals before we head back."

Janie agreed but stipulated that she needed to buy a couple of cases of Sesame Stix. "Is this really the only place you can buy them?"

"No. They're sold in specialty gourmet stores. But the company has fought hard to keep them exclusive. No Walmart contract for them."

"I think I'll give some as gifts. Along with a sketch of this place – it's pretty amazing. Would you mind if I sat and sketched while you take Jake to the zoo?"

"Not at all. We'll play with the jackasses while you draw them."

"Very funny," Janie commented as she dug through her bag for her sketchbook and pen. She opened the book to a clean page and in a few deft strokes captured the lobby, the clowns, the visitors, and the crowd at the glass wall.

She moved closer to the *factory* and quickly sketched the workers, their equipment, and the bags of Sesame Stix.

Jake had finished his drink by the time she returned to their table. She told him to mind Win at the petting zoo. She went first to the cash register at the front of the building to make her purchase, then to a bench outside. A fresh page from her sketchbook soon was filled with a fairly detailed sketch of the building, signs, and balloons.

Then she moved to the petting zoo where she captured Win holding Jake up high enough to pet the head of a mule. "Jackass!" she mouthed at him.

She was pleased with her efforts. She wasn't sure what she'd do with them yet, but the exercise of drawing felt good. Tiring but good.

Win and Jake joined her as she went inside to collect her purchases before going to the van. Jake waved goodbye to each clown he saw before he would climb back into his special seat to watch the remainder of his movie.

Janie squeezed Win's arm as he helped her into the van, "Thank you. That was quite an experience." She shuffled through her bag as he climbed into his seat. Then she held out a brightly colored cellophane package. "Can I interest you in some Sesame Stix?" she said with a wink.

Ruth used the quiet afternoon to dig through her notebooks and the photos and emails she'd stored on her laptop. Talking with Gerry the other night had given her an idea. She had tons of raw materials for a travel memoir or fictional account set in some interesting location where she'd traveled – China, Malaysia, Thailand, Singapore, Korea, etc.

She wasn't sure she wanted to write anything herself – she really didn't think she had the aptitude – but she could collaborate with Gerry, who did. She knew that Gerry was busy with the BellWhether piece, but that wouldn't last forever. She'd talk to Gerry about it. See if she was interested.

In fact, maybe she'd just drive over to Edith for a late lunch and talk to Gerry now. She didn't have anything else she had to do.

At nearly three-fifteen, the diner was empty except for Gerry sitting at a table with a glass of iced tea and her feet propped in a chair. "I'm so glad you're not busy," Ruth said as she joined Gerry at the table. "I want to talk to you about an idea I had."

Gerry offered Ruth a glass of tea, then sat back to listen. Ruth pulled out her notebooks and copies of some photos and emails she'd printed off her laptop. She described to Gerry the other materials she had and the untold, unwritten stories she had in her head. Gerry's level of interest increased as Ruth listed the places she'd been and the things she'd done.

"Anyway," Ruth said at last, "I was wondering if you'd be interested in collaborating with me on something – memoir, fiction, travelogue, or something. After you finish the BellWhether piece, of course."

Gerry looked wide-eyed. "Ruth, you are amazing. My mind is whirling, thinking of the possibilities. Yes, I'd love to work with you and see what we could come up with. I think I've got two or three months left on the BellWhether project, if Belle and Sally like it. But after that…Yes."

"Great! I'll tell you what. While you finish your project, I'll organize my materials. And try to write some of the stories still in my head. Then they'll be ready when you are."

"Ruth, you made my day! Thank you for your confidence in me." She gave Ruth a hug as Ruth gathered her materials to leave.

"I'm excited. I'm going to start right away. And, Gerry? Don't worry. Sally and Belle will love your work." Ruth nearly floated out of the diner.

Gerry closed her eyes for a minute, "Thank you, God. Now for Belle and Sally…."

Ruth arrived home at the same time as Win, Janie, and Jake. Jake was full of news of the day. He danced around her describing blue and red people making sticks. She couldn't keep up with him and was too distracted to try. She told Janie she'd already eaten and needed a nap. But she really just wanted to savor her conversation with Gerry. "God, give me patience," she said softly as she tried to extricate herself from a highly excited Jake. "Don't let me smack him."

Gerry spent Sunday morning typing, proofing, editing, and printing the four chapters of ***BellWhether Tails***. She made two copies, one for each of them, to take with her.

The butterflies in her stomach sent her dashing to the bathroom several times. She replayed her conversation with Ruth over and over, calming herself down with the knowledge that somebody liked her writing. Self-soothing, that was it. She practiced self-soothing with remembered praise.

By the time she arrived at the kennel, she was less nervous than she had been earlier. Maybe Janie's praise idea really did work. She bucked up, took a deep breath, told herself she wrote beautifully, smiled at her silliness, and opened the door to the office.

Sally was waiting for her, inviting her back to the house. Belle had a pitcher of lemonade sitting on the table in front of her. Gerry hugged each of them before sitting across the table from them.

"I've been working on something again that I want to talk with you about." She had their full attention. "Ever since I worked here in high school, I've been fascinated by the stories you told of getting started in your business. I made notes and tried to write down your stories for high school English."

Belle and Sally looked at each other before Belle said, "Surely we're not that interesting."

"You were to me. Are to me. And I think you will be to others. That's why, when I found my old notebooks as I packed to move back here, I decided to try again to write those stories." She held out a folder to each of them.

"I've written four of your stories so far. I want you to read them then talk with me again. I've got some ideas, but I want you to have read them first. Will you?"

Sally said, "Of course. I can't wait." She looked at Belle, who nodded. "When do you want to talk again?"

"How about tomorrow night after I close the diner? About nine?"

Belle agreed, "That will be fine, Gerry. I am amazed that you've done this." She opened the folder and started to read. "Oh, Sally. Wait until you see. Gran and Gramps...."

Sally flipped open her folder and read a bit before looking up with a grin, "What a treat, Gerry. Now go home and let us read!" Her huge smile took the sting out of her dismissal. As she walked to her car, Gerry realized they'd actually paid her a compliment.

"Thank you, God," she whispered. "And thank you Janie and Ruth."

Nine

"Art is for practice between two and three o'clock; not for performance."

Velma Lee Lewis

Gerry woke early the next morning in a state of high nervousness. She had to get herself together for work. Jess bumped her cold nose into Gerry's calf twice before she noticed. "Right, Jess. A little Frisbee game ought to calm me down." Gerry had installed lights in her yard when she'd first moved in so that she and Jess could play after dark. They worked before dawn, too.

Running through the yard with Jess, being silly, did much to calm down the stomach butterflies. After fifteen minutes, Gerry was ready to get on with her day. How had Jess known what she needed? She puzzled about dog's intuition as she jumped in the shower.

She hurriedly got herself ready for another day at the diner and was in her car a minute or two earlier than usual. As she turned the key, her cell phone rang. She jumped – why was the car ringing? In another second she realized her error. Cell phone.

She backed the car to the end of the drive as she fumbled for her phone. It had stopped ringing before she found it. Oh, well, it could wait until she got to the diner. She needed to concentrate on driving.

She put the car in reverse and started to roll out of the driveway when someone ran behind her. Turning her head to look, she nearly twisted her neck off watching Hal King run down the street.

"Prince!" she called as he passed her on the other side of the street. He waved and kept running. The wires from his earbuds flapped against his chest. "Prince jogging? There must be sunspots or something," she mumbled to herself as she turned the car toward Edith.

She arrived at the diner, hurried inside, started the large urn of coffee, and checked her cell phone to see who had called her at that ungodly hour of the morning. Bea.

She hit the call button and the speaker button on her cell phone before laying it on the counter beside her. She needed to work while she talked.

Bea answered on the first ring. "Are you getting tired of early mornings and long days?" she asked.

Gerry sighed, "Boy, I'll say. I don't know how you do it. I'm worn out and it's only been a couple weeks."

Bea chuckled, "I'm glad to hear you say that. I get to feeling old and lazy when I'm totally worn out by Sunday. But the reason I'm calling is to tell you I'll be home this evening. You can sleep in tomorrow morning; I'll take the early shift. But if you could come in around ten-thirty and stay until two or so, that would let me get my house in order before I start back full-time on Wednesday."

"Sure, that would be fine. I've got to go now. My first customer just walked in. See you tomorrow. Have a safe trip." She hung up and sang out a cheery "Good morning!" as she picked up the coffee pot and bustled into the dining room, nearly colliding with Hal King.

"Prince. Twice in one day? Are you stalking me?"

He lifted his sunglasses to peer at her. "Just wanted a cup of coffee so I thought I'd run over."

"Literally? Did you run all the way here?" she asked with a frown. "I would have given you a ride."

"It's okay. I wanted the exercise. And I wanted to talk to you. Can you have a cup of coffee with me?" He turned over another cup at the place across the table from where he'd sat.

"I guess so. Until someone else comes in." She poured herself come coffee and sat across from him at the table closest to the door. "OK. Talk."

Hal took off his sunglasses and looked at her with his intense blue eyes. "I am sorry about blowing you off before. I got scared. We were getting too serious, and I didn't know how to handle it."

"Um-hmm," Gerry fiddled with a spoon, picking it up and laying it down.

"I've grown up in the last five years. I'm not the lazy, spoiled, egotistical ass I was then. At least most days." He gave her a tentative grin.

"Um-hmm." She picked up a fork in her other hand, tapped them both on the rim of the table in a terrible imitation of playing drums.

"I've even started making something of myself. I sold a few songs and bought a little cabin in the mountains. Near Frasier."

"Really? You sold some of your songs? Good for you, Prince!" Gerry gave him a genuine smile.

"I'm going to be at Mom's another week or so. Could I take you out to dinner before I leave? I hear there's a new place over in Buffalo."

"That would be nice. I'd like that." She moved her hand to cover his, but the door opened to Red and two of his rancher buddies.

"Hey, Gerry. Better get busy feeding us or I'll tell Bea you've been slacking," Red announced with a gleam in his eye.

Gerry stood up, picking up the coffee pot. "Thanks, Prince. Give me a call." She turned to Red and friends, "Oh, sit down. I'll bring your coffee. You guys are a real pain, you know it?" Red grinned at her reaction. He loved to tease and be teased.

When Gerry came out of the kitchen with a fresh pot of coffee, Hal was gone. A five dollar bill lay by his plate. On it was a napkin on which he'd written, "Friday, six-thirty?" She tucked the money and napkin into her pocket and got on with her day.

Bea pulled up at the kennel about five o'clock that evening. She was tired from the drive back from northwest Arkansas, but happy to be home. Her first stop would be to pick up Shep, then she'd go see what shape her house was in. Seth had sent her an email that he was finished with the cleanup. She hoped so. She just wanted to be in her own home.

Sally had seen Bea drive up and came outside to greet her. "Well, Wayfarer. Welcome home." She gave Bea a hug, saying "I hope your trip was successful."

Bea hugged her back. "Thanks, I'm glad to be home." She looked into the office, "Is Belle here?"

"Yes, she's out with the dogs, but she should be about done. You want to go spring Shep then find Belle?"

Bea agreed and fell into step next to Sally. "I'm hoping to talk the two of you into going with me to see my house. I'm feeling rather apprehensive about it."

"We can ask her. I can go, but I have to be back before seven for a call I need to take with a sheriff's office in Oregon."

They saw Belle working with a young border collie and a high school student wearing a BellWhether t-shirt. "No, it's not too soon to start training a puppy. You can teach them the basic obedience commands – come, sit, down, stay – when they're still very young as long as you do it slowly and make it fun and possible for them to succeed. Here, give me one of those treats."

The girl handed Belle a soft round dog cookie. Belle crumbled it into many small pieces. "Now watch."

She moved away from the puppy by two or three steps and called his name in a high, excited voice, "Runner, come!" When he came, she gave him a treat. If he didn't come, she simply ignored him.

"I'm giving him choices," she told the new kennel helper. "If he chooses correctly he gets rewarded, If not, he gets ignored." She went through the exercise twice more, this time getting his compliance both times. "See, if you let him choose, he'll learn faster than if you coerce him into obedience. Let his actions seem to be his idea. Set up boundaries, if you have to, to keep him from failing. Then give him the freedom to choose. And don't 'no' him to death. Save that powerful word for stopping something dangerous."

The girl looked blank. Too much information.

"I think he's had enough today. We want to keep this fun." She picked up the puppy and handed it to the girl. "Would you put him back in his run, please?" The girl carried the puppy off while Belle gave Bea a hug.

"Belle, are you available to go with me to see my house? I'm feeling anxious about it. I'd like you two to come with me."

Belle patted her shoulder. "Yes, I can go. Just let me wash up."

As they walked to the office, the three friends chatted about the girl Belle had been working with. "Bradley King's cousin," Belle said, "but not nearly as ambitious or motivated as he."

"I think he's been helping Seth work on your house nearly every day," Sally reported. "I can't wait to see what they've done."

When they arrived at Bea's house, Ruth and Jake were walking by. "Out for a little walk before dinner," Ruth called after welcoming Bea home. "Jake's escorting me." She patted the top of his head. "Did you have a good trip?" she asked Bea, who nodded and smiled.

"Come on, Aunt Ruthie. I walk-ded. Now let's eat! I'm hungry!" Jake demanded.

"I'll call you later," Ruth promised as she hurried after Jake, who'd taken off at a gallop.

Belle and Sally had walked up to the kitchen door while Bea visited with Ruth. Sally tried the door, and it opened easily. She looked inside and gasped.

"What? What's wrong?" Bea asked, pushing past Sally into the house. "Oh, my!" she exclaimed as she looked around. "Oh, my goodness!"

It was beautiful. The cabinets had been stripped of their old white paint to expose golden oak varnished to a high gloss. The Formica counter top that was charred and melted next to the stove had been replaced with chocolate brown granite.

Someone, Bradley she guessed, had washed and put away all the dishes, groceries, pots and pans. The appliances were all sparkling. The walls had been painted cream and the trim white.

It was bright, clean, and ready to use.

Bea sat at the refinished oak table in a refinished oak chair. "I had no idea this table and chairs could look this good. I'm nearly speechless." She smoothed her hand over the warmly glowing tabletop. Her other hand brushed away a tear.

"I think you can safely plan to stay here tonight," Belle said. She'd walked through the rest of the house and seen the results of similar efforts everywhere. "They really did a bang up job!"

Bea nodded, brushing away another tear. "I am very lucky." She walked through the house, exclaiming over the fresh paint and cleaned floors, curtains, and furniture. "I really can't believe they did all this so fast!" When she returned to the kitchen, Sally had made a pot of tea.

"Sit down and let it soak in, Bea," Sally suggested.

Bea sat, took a sip of tea, and sighed. "Let me tell you about my trip another time. Right now I'm just overwhelmed with my house."

Sally and Bea stayed only another few minutes. As they left, Bea hugged them again and thanked them for boarding Shep. "I'm going back to work tomorrow," she informed them. "I've got some changes to make there, too."

Shep brought a ball and placed it in her lap. "OK, boyo. Let's go through the ritual of coming home. It's important to claim our places again." She threw the ball. Shep fetched it. They were home.

At shortly after nine o'clock that night, Gerry again tapped on the kennel office door. This time Belle welcomed her and led her back to the house. "It's such a pleasant evening, we thought we'd sit on the porch," Belle told her as she opened the door to the large screened porch where Sally was already seated flipping through Gerry's folder.

Belle took a seat in her big rocker and picked up her copy of the folder. "First off, Gerry, we want you to know how much we like what you've done. I could just hear Sally's voice telling her stories."

Sally added, "And you got almost all the facts straight. I marked a couple little things, but I'm really amazed. You must have taken copious notes."

Gerry felt herself blush. "I took a lot. Anytime either of you talked about your past, I wrote it down."

"Well, Belle and I both love what you've done. You said you had some other ideas?"

"Here it is," Gerry thought, "time to put my best foot forward, my cards on the table. Why am I thinking in clichés?" She took a breath then spoke out loud, "I'd like to turn these stories into a book. I mean a real book – in print and as an ebook, distributed by Amazon, Barnes and Noble, and other online retailers as well as local businesses. I think it would also promote your business. People want to do business with people they like. I think they'll like you very much after reading this book.

"But it's not long enough. I need to have a story about how Sally got shot, and one about how you came to Plainview. If I'm going to finish this project, I'll need to interview you both and listen to your stories." She looked at each of them. They were with her so far.

"The problem is that I really need to earn some money. My proposition is this – would you be willing to fund me while I finish the book? That means writing, editing, publishing, and getting it into distribution channels. And publicizing it after it's published."

Sally and Belle looked at each other for a moment. Belle said, "Won't you have to find an agent and a publisher? That makes the enterprise fairly uncertain. Oh, I don't mean it won't be good, but lots of good stuff doesn't get published, and lots of crap does. Or so I've heard."

Gerry responded quickly, "You're right. That's why I think we should self-publish. We won't be dependent on anyone else. We can set up a subsidiary company, BellWhether Books, for example. And run all the publishing expenses through it. All profits would channel through it, too. That will keep everything separate from the kennel business and easy to track.

"We can split the royalties for the sales. I'd even be willing to deduct what you pay me for finishing the book from future royalties."

"What kind of publishing expense are we looking at?" Sally asked. "And how many copies do we have to buy?"

Gerry grinned, "Nothing and none. We can do print-on-demand production of the book so that we only pay for a book when we order it. And there are no minimums. We could print only the proof copy and quit, paying for just the production of one book."

"And how much is that? If we have to pay a lot for each copy, where's the profit?" Belle's interest was definitely piqued.

"The cost will depend on the style and size of the book for print copies – paperback is much less expensive than hardbound, for example, and larger books cost more than smaller ones, considering both page count and physical size.

"Ebooks cost pennies to produce. But we'll need distribution channels and online retailers. Our profit will be split with them.

"We set the prices, so we can add on whatever we want to the production cost, as long as we stay in the ballpark for similar books. And we also set the wholesale prices, although it is customary to give forty or fifty percent off retail price to wholesale customers. Setting the prices will be an interesting exercise."

"What about promotion? Won't that cost a lot of money?" Belle asked, making notes on a pad in front of her.

"Well, it can. But it doesn't have to. Advertise it in your newsletter. Do a book signing at the kennel as part of any event you hold. Go to border collie and bloodhound specialties and take the books along." Gerry had done her research. It showed.

"Bottom line," asked Belle, "what would our monetary risk be?"

Gerry had thought about this question, too. "My wages to finish the book. I'll work for three hundred dollars a week. I think I can finish in two to three months. So $2500 - $3500 is a fair guess."

"That's cheap wages," Sally commented. "Can you get by on so little? It's just barely minimum wage for a forty-hour week. And I'm sure you'll put in more than forty hours."

"Yes, I will. But I'll settle for forty. I can get by on that for a short time. And I'm betting on a bigger reward later from my share of the royalties."

"I don't want to split the royalties with you," Sally surprised Gerry by saying. "I'd like to recover our investment and let you have all the rest of the royalties. You're the one doing all the work."

"But it's your intellectual capital," Gerry reminded them.

"It's like gold buried in my back yard. It's not worth much of anything if someone doesn't dig it up." Sally gave Belle a slight nod.

"OK, Gerry. We'll pay you up to $3,500 for a completed book, published, and available for distribution." Belle referred to her notes, "We will subtract our investment amount from the royalties due to you. All other royalties are yours. That ought to be a good incentive to do some promotion." She laughed.

"There's only one hitch," Gerry said. "I need some story-time with you two. The sooner, the better."

"I've got some time tomorrow afternoon. Will that do?" Sally volunteered.

Gerry agreed. They all shook hands. Then Gerry found her way home. She wasn't sure how. Her head had been in the clouds for the entire trip.

The next afternoon, Gerry spent two hours with Sally, drinking iced tea, listening, and taking notes as Sally told about Dusty, the best dog she ever had – or at least one of them.

BellWhether Tails
Dusty – 1984

Nosy turned ten the year I got Dusty. I hadn't thought I'd ever find a better mantrailer than Nosy, but I hadn't yet met Dusty.

Dusty was three years old when Jo Beth called and asked if I had room for another dog. She wanted to place Dusty somewhere well away from Georgia. He'd trailed a jail breaker, alerted the K-9 "bite" dogs, and watched with Jo Beth as the joint law enforcement posse took the well-disguised prisoner back into custody. As they loaded the jail breaker into the sheriff's car, he screamed that he would kill that damned ugly dog.

Jo Beth took no chances with her dogs. She'd had several offers for Dusty, but she wanted him where she knew he'd be used and treated well. I agreed to take him.

I talked it over with my boss, the sheriff of Ford County. I knew he didn't have the budget for another dog. "I'll keep him and handle him. If we use him in an official search, you can pay me an hourly rate for the dog." He agreed.

I had one run left in my half of the kennel, so I put Dusty next to Nosy. I hoped she might teach him something through proximity. She really was that good – she'd helped me train dogs for the last eight years.

I started training Dusty the day after I got him, or rather, training myself about his way of trailing. It's individual to each dog, and the handler needs to figure out the "tells" of her dog. Nosy, for example, always shook her head at least twice when she headed in a wrong direction and corrected herself.

Anyway, Dusty hadn't been with me more than a month when a child went missing. I sent Doug McAllister out with one of Nosy's offspring, Sniffs, an accomplished veteran with many successes under his harness. I took Dusty to see how he'd do in a real situation.

He was amazing. Not only could he trail, but he made sure to signal to me what he was doing. I'd never seen anything like it. Then when he belly-crawled up to the terrified child and let her hug his big neck, all of us had tears in our eyes. After that, Bell accused me of including the word *Dusty* in every sentence I spoke. She was right: I was totally smitten.

I had to force myself to work anyone but Dusty. I was training three young dogs for delivery to law enforcement agencies in Illinois — they came to me. I had never imagined when I first went to the swamps of Georgia ten years ago that I would become a well-respected breeder and trainer of bloodhounds.

In fact, my popularity exceeded my capabilities. I had a long waiting list of law enforcement organizations that wanted one of my dogs. But to increase the number of dogs I had available, I would have to quit working for the sheriff's office and train dogs full-time. And I'd have to get bigger facilities. As it was, I had to time the whelping of litters to the graduation of trained dogs to ensure I had enough kennel space.

Bell was in almost the same spot. She'd won nearly every trial west of the Mississippi and east of the Rockies. Her pups, trained and untrained, were in great demand both as working dogs on farms and ranches and as participants in the growing sport of herding trials.

Nearly every county fair throughout the central states had a rodeo. And nearly every rodeo sponsored herding trials in the same arena where cowboys got bounced off bulls. Bell had won accolades and jackpots worth thousands of dollars over her years of competition.

Doug had become a hell of a handler, too. Of course he had great dogs to work with. The dogs had such a reputation that Bell and Doug had trouble getting others to compete against them.

Once when Doug was just getting started, he went to a trial without Bell. He took Chester, one of the Gunsmoke clan (progeny of either Miss Kitty or Dillon), and a younger and untested dog, Chance, with him. He crated Chester and took Chance along to enter the competition. He'd scruffed up Chance so that he looked ungroomed and pretty wild. Nobody knew Doug, and his dog didn't look like much, so he got invited to enter the big jackpot trial worth $1000. He accepted, paid the entry fee, and disappeared with his dog until time for the trial.

When he came to the arena to compete he had Chester, not Chance, with him. Chester beat the collars off all the competition. Doug pulled that same trick several times, bought himself a car with the winnings, and never called Chester anything but "Ringer" after that first outing.

Bell apparently spent more time thinking about how we could make more money than I did. One day she came to me with spreadsheets showing projected earnings and potential revenues from expansion.

"I've been playing with numbers. I think we could retire from our jobs and live off our dog business in five years if we start saving for it now." She pointed out her calculations and explained her projections.

I agreed with her that it looked possible. "OK. We'll have to cut back some on our expenses to save enough, but I'm game to try."

Bell drew up a chart that she posted in the kennel building showing our starting point and our goal. She said she'd update it every month so we'd have a visual record of our savings.

I smiled at her organized approach. I'd probably just stick dollar bills in a coffee can if it were up to me.

Everything was on target for the first six months. In fact we saved even more than she'd projected by buying feed in bulk. Ten percent off the cost of dog food when you're feeding at least eighteen dogs (not counting puppies) is not an inconsiderable amount. We were excited and proud as Bell charted the sixth consecutive rise in the line that headed upward to our goal.

To celebrate, we decided to stay in town after work and have dinner out. It had been six months since we'd eaten dinner at a restaurant — we'd cut that out as part of our austerity measures. We had a nice meal at a moderately-priced café and drove home feeling good about ourselves and our progress.

When we got to the ranch, the dogs were all barking and howling. The spotlights on the south side of the kennel were not lighting the driveway as they usually did. I felt a clutch of fear grip my stomach — something was wrong.

Bell got a flashlight out of the glove box, and I positioned the truck so its headlights shown into the kennel yard. Bell led the way as we loped across the field to see what was going on. I saw it first. The chain link fence had been cut in the southwest corner pen. The fencing was partially rolled back to create a hole big enough for a person to get through.

I tapped Bell on the shoulder and pointed at the fence. I held a finger to my lips – we needed to be quiet. Someone might have crawled through the flap-door and be inside the building. I went back to the truck for my service revolver that I kept locked in a box bolted behind the seat. I motioned for Bell to stay still until I got back. Dog-training hand signals work with people, too.

When I got back I whispered in her ear to go up to the house and call for emergency backup while I patrolled the area. If she drove the truck away, maybe our intruder would think we'd left. She did as I asked while I walked around enough to see glass lying on the ground from the broken-out spot lights. Then I stood in the shadows and watched. I used my peripheral vision, a skill I'd learned doing night trailing and stakeouts.

Someone or something crawled out the flap-door and moved along the edge of the building. I waited. I wanted to be sure of what I thought I saw. Then with a quick dash, the person was slipping out the opening of the fence as I called out, "Halt! Sheriff's department."

The runner turned toward me and charged me. I'd made a stupid mistake in not keeping the flashlight so I could blind the runner with a beam of strong light in his eyes. As I hesitated about drawing my weapon, he knocked me down and ran to the trees.

I felt such a fool! I had just got back on my feet when Bell arrived back at my side. "I'm going after the crazy bastard!" I cried. "He's nuts! Ran right into me. Lucky I didn't shoot him!"

Bell grabbed my arm. "Slow down, Sal. You don't want to go flying after him in a rage. Into the woods. By yourself."

I stared at her in exasperation. She was right, dammit, but I wanted to catch the crazy bastard. I started to tell her just that when I thought I saw movement in the corner yard. I grabbed the flashlight and swung it around to sweep its high beam across the yard. I caught a flash of white on the ground against the building near the flap-door. I walked toward it and hit it with my light again. It was something, but I couldn't tell what.

I turned off the flashlight to keep from making myself a bigger target and crept forward. "I have a gun pointing right at you!" I yelled. "Don't move or I'll shoot." I zigzagged across the field and slid through the fence. I listened closely but could hear only dogs barking inside the building.

I took a deep breath, dropped to the ground, steadied my gun and switched on the flashlight again, pointing it where I'd seen the figure before. Lying on the ground next to the flap-door was a girl, tied up in yellow rope with a gag duct-taped in her mouth.

"Bell," I hollered as I knelt next to the girl, "Come. Now." I felt for a pulse and found one, steady and strong if too rapid. I realized she was conscious, just scared stiff.

"It's okay, honey. You're safe. I'm a deputy sheriff. I'll take care of you. Hang on a little while longer." I found a corner of the duct tape covering her mouth. "This will probably hurt," I told her as I jerked the tape off. She whimpered, and I saw tears stream from her eyes.

Bell had arrived and worked with me to loosen the ropes and calm the girl. I left them to run into the building, through the flap-door, to find a knife for the stubborn ropes. While inside, I flipped on the lights and saw the chaos our friend had made – papers dumped from drawers, Bell's chart ripped in pieces, and bins of dog food dumped on the floor. At least all the dogs seemed to be okay.

After opening the exterior door and gate I hurried back to cut the girl's ropes, and between us Bell and I carried her inside and set her on a chair that Bell righted.

"Are you okay?" Bell asked gently as she took the girl's hand and smoothed its back with her thumb.

She nodded, wiping the tears from her face with one hand and holding onto Bell with the other.

"I'll be right back," I told them. I picked up the phone to call the sheriff's office, but had no dial tone. The crazy bastard had pulled the wire out of the wall. "Bell, I'm going to the house to call again. See if you can find out what happened."

By the time I got back, Bell was sitting next to the girl, holding her close and smoothing her hair. "Sally, this is Robin Brown. We need to let her parents know that she's all right. She's been away from home since early this morning." Bell intentionally kept her voice calm and her tone gentle. She squeezed Robin's shoulder as she spoke.

"Why don't you two go up to the house so you can call Robin's parents. This phone seems to be broken. And Bell, maybe you can get Robin something to eat while we wait for the other deputies to get here. I'll bet she's hungry." Robin gave me a small smile.

"I'm going to get Dusty out to see if he can find a trail." She started to interrupt, but I held up a hand. "No, I won't go anywhere until backup gets here." She raised an eyebrow. "I promise."

In the fifteen minutes before the sheriff's car arrived, I had checked on every dog thoroughly and had gotten Dusty into his harness and ready to trail.

I quickly explained the situation to the two deputies, Jeff and Greg. I sent Jeff to take Robin's statement, and got Greg ready to back me up as we trailed the kidnapper through the woods.

I didn't hold much hope that we'd find anyone. Twenty minutes was an eternity in a chase, but I had to try. Dusty seemed to sense my urgency and took off toward the trees at a gallop.

I followed behind him, yelling at Greg to try to keep up. Dusty did not hesitate or self-correct. He just very deliberately moved quickly forward. I held his thirty-foot long lead in one hand and the flashlight in the other. I tried to shine the light just ahead of where I stepped so I could avoid tripping over a rock or tree root. At the rate we were traveling, paying attention to my feet and Dusty's movements took all my concentration.

Suddenly three things happened almost simultaneously – Dusty launched himself at a diagonal from the direction he'd been heading, a shot rang out, and my left leg collapsed underneath me, sending me backwards into oblivion.

It took me a long time to piece together what had happened after I blacked out. Morphine tends to erase some things and distort others. It was sometime after my first surgery before I could retain anything that anyone told me. I think by then they'd lowered my dose.

"Bell, I think I've asked you this before, but tell me again. How did I hurt my knee?"

She gave me a sad smile. I knew she must have told me before, probably several times. I didn't even know how much time she spent at the hospital with me. She was there every time I looked for her.

"Sally, tell me what you remember," Bell said patiently. "I'll pick it up from there."

"I remember Dusty lunging at something, the sound of a shot and my leg collapsing. I guess I got shot in the leg – the knee. But I don't know who shot me or what happened afterward."

"Do you remember Robin Brown, the girl we found outside the kennel building?"

"I think so. But I don't know why she was there."

She studied me intently. "I can tell you a little or a lot. But I'm only going to tell you a little if you're going to forget it again."

"How can I tell? I don't know what I'll forget."

Bell scrunched her lips together. "OK. Here's a plan. I'll tell you a little, then check back with you in a couple hours and see if you remember. If you do, I'll tell you more."

"What if I remember it for a few hours then forget?"

"I guess we'll figure that out if we have to." She took a deep breath. "Dusty saved your life. He jumped on the man who shot you and knocked his arm down so that he shot you in the knee instead of the head or heart." She relaxed her tense face into a little smile. "Let's see if you can remember that for a while."

I was shocked. I guess I thought my shattered knee was the result of an accident, not an intentional attempt to hurt me. Bell patted my shoulder, "I've got to take care of some errands. I'll be back in a couple hours. We'll talk more then."

While she was gone, I concentrated on remembering that Dusty saved my life. That sweet boy saved my life.

As Bell walked through the door to my room, I told her with a smile, "Dusty saved my life. Now tell me more."

She poured herself some water from my pitcher and sat in the only chair in the room. She made herself as comfortable as she could and started talking.

"Greg was right behind you during your dash into the woods. He heard the shot and saw you fall. He didn't know whether the shooter would try again so he crept quietly to you. He saw you'd been shot in the knee. You were unconscious and bleeding. But he thought he should leave you to find the shooter.

"He said he heard growling before he saw anything. Dusty was standing on top of the man, holding him down by the throat."

I interrupted, "Dusty was? He doesn't have an aggressive bone in his body."

"Except where you're concerned, I guess. Anyway, Greg announced himself, read the man his rights, told him not to move or he'd shoot, and pulled Dusty out of the way. He said he nearly lost it when he looked down into the bloodied face of J.D. McAllister."

"Damn! I *knew* it was J.D. I've been after him for twenty years. Double damn!" I was shouting when a nurse stuck her head in the door and told Bell not to excite the patient.

"Sorry. Maybe we better continue this later," Bell told me after the nurse left.

"Not on your life," I fired back. "Talk."

Bell grinned at me as she continued, "Greg cuffed McAllister to a tree and took the gun and Dusty with him. He stopped to check on you. Dusty sniffed you, licked your face, and lay down beside you. Refused to move. Greg knew he needed to get you the hospital and wondered how to alert Jeff without leaving you alone when he heard sirens. More backup had arrived.

"He told Dusty to stay with you. He followed the broken branches out of the woods where he found the other deputies waiting. He told one to radio for an ambulance while he and the other assembled the portable stretcher from the car's trunk. Before the ambulance arrived, they had you out of the woods. Dusty wouldn't leave your side. McAllister was cuffed and sitting in one of the sheriff's cars."

"Then J.D. walked up."

"What?" I yelled. "What did you say?"

"I said that J.D walked up," she repeated slowly.

"I thought you said J.D. was the shooter and was cuffed in the car. Oh, damn. I'm losing it. I guess you'll have to tell me this again. I'm forgetting."

"No, you're okay. You didn't forget. That's what I said."

"Dammit, Bell. Don't screw with me!"

"I'm not, Sal. Greg thought he'd captured J.D. McAllister. But he'd captured J.D.'s brother, D.J."

"You are making that up!" I held my volume down, but Bell knew I was hollering.

"Turns out J.D. and D.J. look a lot alike. But D.J. has always been in trouble – in school, with the law, in jail. He wasn't around here much over the last twenty years. But we'd run into him before."

"The peeping tom!" I was aghast.

"Yeah. And Gramps' attacker."

"But why, Bell? Why did he want to mess with us?" I searched her face for an answer.

"I don't know. J.D. said he didn't know either. He only knew that every time D.J. got out of jail, he headed here to think up new ways to harass us. J.D. tried to reason with him, tried to order him never to come back, even reported him to his parole board. But D.J. kept coming back. For some reason, he'd decided he hated us."

"Oh my God! All those years I've thought it was J.D. and all along he was trying to protect us." I shook my head several times. "What was D.J. trying to do this time?"

Bell took a drink of water. "You've got to understand that he's crazy. I mean really crazy."

"OK."

"He kidnapped Robin Brown as she was walking to school. He planned to take her into our kennel building, rape and kill her, and wait for us to find her. Then he'd do the same to us." Bell's face paled as she grimly reported the facts.

"Robin said he kept muttering about finally showing those bitches. And screaming, 'You bitches! You'll pay! You'll finally pay!' She said he screamed it at her, out the window as he was driving, and at the building when he arrived."

"Good God! That poor child. She must have been terrified."

"Yes. Luckily we got home when we did."

Tears streamed down my face. "I guess we saved her, didn't we?" Bell nodded. "And Dusty saved me."

"Yes, Sally. Thank God!"

I lay back and closed my eyes. I was exhausted. "Thank you for telling me."

"Rest now, Sal. Remember that we saved Robin. And Dusty saved you. Then let the rest of it go."

I nodded agreement. She was right. But I knew I couldn't do it yet. It would take a couple of dog-lives before I didn't wake up angry every morning.

Ten

"Don't invite new people into your home until you've known them for at least three months."
Velma Lee Lewis

Win stood at Janie's door, nervously bouncing from foot to foot. When she answered the door, he backed up a step, grinned, and made a show of looking her up and down. "Playing in your mommy's makeup, little girl?" he asked with a grin.

Janie turned a puzzled face up to him, "What?" He reached to her face, rubbed her cheek with his thumb, and held up the thumb for her inspection. Blue.

She rolled her eyes. "I got into it again?" She held out her hands, one of which sported a large orange smudge. "Damn," she shrugged.

Win chuckled. "It looks cute on you. I just stopped by to see if you were busy this evening. I want to make you a proposition."

"Really?" she waggled her eyebrows. "Come on in," she led the way into the kitchen where she picked up her abandoned glass of tea and offered him one.

He nodded as he looked around for the source of a childish voice he could hear somewhere near. Janie watched him swivel his head and guessed its cause. "Down there," she pointed.

Win followed her finger to look into the next room where he saw a chair covered with a blanket and a small foot sticking out from under the blanket's edge. "Ah," he sighed.

"So what's your proposition?" Janie asked as she handed him a glass of tea.

"I'll show you mine if you show me yours." Win announced. He'd thought up the line as he walked to her house, but the look on her face silenced him.

"My what?" Janie demanded.

"Your paintings." Win's sheepish look softened Janie's expression.

"You paint?"

"No. You do."

Janie rolled her eyes again. "I know. But what's your trade? If I show you my paintings, what will you show me?"

"Oh. My gardens." Win looked abashed. "This isn't going the way I planned. I was trying to be clever, and it backfired." He took a breath, "Let me start over. Janie, I'd like to show you my gardens and see your paintings. Do you have time to do that this evening?" He checked out her expression. "After I take you out for dinner," he threw in.

Janie conceded. "OK. What time?"

"Pick you up at six-thirty? I heard about a new place I'd like to try. That all right with you?"

"Sure." The rueful smile stayed on Janie's face as she escorted him to the door. "Next time, start at the end," she suggested. "See you at six-thirty."

Win walked away, shaking his head at his stupidity. He almost blew it. And he really didn't want to do that.

That evening, Jake waved from the doorway as Janie left with Win, "Bye, Momma." He came inside and announced, "Aunt Ruthie, let's do something fun tonight."

"OK, Jakester. What kind of fun do you want to have? Read a book fun, tell a story fun, watch a movie fun, or play a game fun?"

Jake stuck out his bottom lip as he considered, "Tell a story fun. Your story."

"My story? Don't you want to tell a story?" Ruth turned her head to study Jake.

"Nope. Want you to tell a story."

"Well, OK," Ruth said uncertainly. "I have to think of one. Why don't you get your bath while I think, then I'll tell you a story before you go to sleep. Deal?"

Jake's lip jutted out again as he thought over Ruth's offer. "Don't need a bath."

"The deal's off." Ruth turned to walk away.

"OK. Deal." Jake said, running to the bathroom. "I get to turn on the water."

"Only the cold. I do the hot," Ruth reminded him as she trailed him down the hall.

While Jake was in the tub, Ruth shuffled through the keepsakes she had dug out to show Gerry. She found a Malaysian shadow puppet made from leather. The head, trunk, and legs were mounted on a stick. The arms were attached with brads to the shoulders, and the elbows were hinged. Sticks attached to hands let the puppet gesture. Details of the face were cut out of the leather. Held in front of a light source, the puppet cast fantastic shadows. Now if she could only think up a story to go with it.

Suddenly she saw the wavy-bladed *kris*. It was a wooden blunt-edged replica meant for a souvenir letter opener, but it looked dangerous. And magical.

She remembered the old Malay shopkeeper in Kuala Lumpur who'd sold her the kris. He told her that many people believed that the spirits of the blade's previous owners were attached to it. You could talk to the spirits in your dreams if you put the kris under your pillow. Maybe she could come up with a story about the kris without scaring Jake to death.

Fifteen minutes of bubbles and battleships were sufficient for Jake. "I'm clean! I want my story."

Ruth handed him a towel, "Dry off and go get into your jammies. Then I'll tell you a story. Climb in bed. I'll be right there." Ruth went to retrieve her props.

"Not bed yet. The cloud room," he called after her. He'd renamed the dining room since the water spots on the ceiling, like clouds, had figures to be discovered within them.

Ruth got the puppet, the kris, and a desk lamp and carried them into the dining room. She pulled a small table and a chair in from the living room. She put the lamp on the table and pulled the chair up next to it, sat in the chair and turned on the lamp. Holding the shadow puppet in front of the lamp, she made a fantastic figure on the wall opposite. She played with the arm sticks until she was able to move one at a time while holding the puppet stable with the stick in the other hand.

She called Jake in, sat him down in the middle of the room, turned off the ceiling lights, and sat down behind the table. She turned on the desk lamp and told Jake to watch the light on the wall. Then she began in the time-honored way: "Once upon a time...."

Jake was fascinated to see the shadow puppet move across the wall, move its arms and bow its body as Ruth told of the boy's search for a magic sword – a kris of such power that whoever owned it could make all his wishes come true, as long as he wished only for good things. The magic kris was made from a magic serpent turned to steel.

She dodged the shadow puppet through the lamplight until, at last, she held the kris up to the light and let its shadow play across the wall.

"The magic kris," Ruth said, "must never be used for harm. Only for good. And its owner will find joy and happiness. Its final gift to its owner is this: when you sleep with the magic kris under your pillow, you can talk to the magic serpent in your dreams.

"And so, Jake, the magic kris is ready for you. Take it to bed, put it under your pillow, and dream of all the magic waiting for you in your life." With that, Ruth turned out the light and placed the wooden kris in Jake's hands.

"Jake, take care of this kris, and it will give you magic. Be kind to other people and it will bring you joy."

Jake was hypnotized by the spectacle Ruth had produced. He held the kris reverently and walked purposefully to his room. He put the kris under his pillow, made a final trip to the bathroom, and crawled into bed. He hugged Ruth hard around the neck,

"Oh, Aunt Ruthie, that was the bestest story in the world. And don't worry. I'll take care of kris. He can sleep under my pillow and talk to me in my dreams."

Ruth kissed Jake's forehead and smiled as she left his room. She hoped she hadn't overdone it. But then she remembered there is no over-the-top when you're four.

The next morning at breakfast, Janie described her evening to Ruth. "Win's gardens are absolutely lovely. He's built serpentine beds under the huge oak trees and filled them with woodland and shade-loving plants. I'll have to get him to show you. They're spectacular."

"Did he like your illustrations?"

"Yes, he said all the right things. And like Gerry, he got the idea of the homeless wee folk right away."

"That's great. I think that was a great idea of his – to share with each other your creative projects. It's a perfect way to get to know each other better."

Janie grinned, "I like what I'm getting to know." She glared at Ruth in mock severity, "But don't start with the teasing, OK?"

Ruth nodded solemnly, "I'll give you a day's grace."

"Thank you very damned much." She sipped her coffee, "What did you and Jake do last night?"

Ruth told her about the shadow puppet show and the magical kris. Janie had started to ask how Jake liked it when he came charging into the kitchen carrying the kris. "Aunt Ruthie, guess what! Kris told me you're going to get me a puppy. And his name is Oliver."

"Oh. Huh. Wow. So you had a magic dream last night?" Ruth stammered, nonplussed.

"Hey, buster, who's Kris and what are you holding?" Janie asked.

Jake held out the sword for Janie to see. "His name is Kris. He's magic. And he talked to me in my dream last night."

Janie advised, "Maybe you should put Kris back in your room. We don't want it to get hurt."

Jake ran off to put the kris back under his pillow. Janie looked hard at Ruth, "Now what are you going to do? Get him a dog to keep the magic alive or let him be disappointed when you don't? And Oliver? Where did that come from?"

"I don't know. We didn't talk about dogs at all. I guess we'll just have to wait and see what Kris provides." She shrugged, "Don't you believe in magic?"

Just before noon, Ruth was alone in the house. Janie and Jake were in the backyard working on the fort. Win had given Janie some scrap lumber for the endeavor, and Janie was valiantly attempting to nail it into submission. Ruth was sure it had taken seven nails to hold one four-foot long piece of one-by-two to the corner post.

The phone rang as she watched the master carpenters at last succeed in attaching three unparallel cross-pieces to two posts. There was a smile in her voice as she answered the phone.

"It's Bea. What's so funny?"

"I'm standing at the window watching Janie help Jake build a fort." Ruth dared to say no more. She was about to explode into a belly laugh.

"Are you busy later, around one? I've got something to show you. Is it okay if I come by?"

"That'll be fine. I'll be here."

After she hung up, Ruth went back to the window. Jake was holding a small board against the post. He flinched, moving it, every time Janie swung the hammer. She'd yet to hit it. Ruth shook her head in amusement. She'd have to go help; Janie'd run out of nails before she got two more pieces nailed up.

As she went into the bedroom to put on cooler clothes, the phone rang again. "Hello," she answered briskly.

"Ruth? It's Sally."

"Hi, Sally. What's up?"

"Are you going to be home later? We've got an idea we want to run by you. Is it okay if we come by?"

"That's odd. Bea just said the same thing." Ruth noted.

"What?"

"She's going to come by around one."

"Oh, good. We'll catch up with both of you at once."

"Funny that you both said the same words – come by. Doesn't that have something to do with dogs?" Ruth's knowledge of technical dog terms was limited.

"You're right. It's a herding term. Funny we both said it. Well, anyway. We'll see you around one." Sally disconnected without a farewell.

Ruth changed her clothes and went out to help Janie, whose patience was stretched to transparency. "Need another pair of hands?" she asked.

"Yeah, attached to a carpenter," Janie snapped.

Ruth took the hammer from Janie and the board from Jake. She laid the board on the ground and hammered a nail part way into it. She picked up the board, positioned it on the upright post, ordered Janie to hold it steady, and gave the nail two quick slams to set it. "Now back up," she advised. Another two slams and the board was attached.

Janie's mouth dropped open. "Why the heck didn't you tell me you knew how to do that?"

"You didn't ask." She picked up a few more nails from Jake's hand and walked to the other end of the cross piece. She held it against the upright post, laid the level she'd brought out with her on top of the cross piece, adjusted it slightly, tapped in the nail, then slammed it home.

Ruth picked up another nail, tapped it far enough into the wood to hold, then slammed the hammer onto the nail. "Two nails is the minimum to hold a board if you don't want it to be able to rotate around the single nail."

"Wow, Aunt Ruthie. You're good. I bet you could build a sky-scraper." Jake excitedly waved his arms around, sprinkling nails as he did.

"Maybe not a skyscraper, Jake. I don't like heights."

"Bet you could build a short skyscraper," he said loyally.

"Seriously! How do you know how to do that?" Janie demanded, hands on hips.

"Dad taught me. I was his little tag-along as a kid. I used to help him on most of his projects. Haven't swung a hammer in a while, but I guess it's like riding a bike." She rubbed her right bicep with her left hand. "I bet my arm's sore tomorrow."

Janie sulked as she watched Ruth nail up two more boards. "I'm going to fix lunch. Jake, you and Carl the Carpenter come in and eat in a few minutes."

"Who's Carl the Carpenter? Is he going to build my fort? Where is he? I don't see him." Jake whirled around looking for someone.

"Never mind, Jake. Your momma's trying to be funny. Let's nail up these last boards and go in for lunch."

After they'd eaten tuna fish sandwiches with a layer of potato chips between the tuna and the bread – Jake-style – Ruth hurried to make a pitcher of iced tea and clean up the kitchen.

"Expecting company?" Janie asked.

"Oh, I forgot to tell you. Both Bea and Sally called to say they're going to come by. Don't you think that's odd?"

"What's odd about them coming to visit?"

"No, that they said they wanted to come by. Come by. It's a herding term."

"What's it mean?"

Ruth shrugged. "I forgot to ask. But they both said it, and I think that's odd." She huffed off to her bedroom to change clothes again. She had just sat down at her computer to use Google to find herding terms when the doorbell rang.

All of her guests were standing on the porch together. Belle was holding something in her arms. Ruth invited everyone inside, and went to fetch the tea pitcher and glasses. As she handed out the glasses, she saw that Belle was holding a black and white mottled dog. "Who's your friend?" she asked.

"Not mine. Yours, I thought. He was sitting on the walk in front of your house and followed us onto your porch. I thought he belonged to you, so I brought him in."

"I've never seen him before. Sort of a strange-looking border collie, isn't he? What color do you call that?" She petted the puppy's head as she spoke.

"He's not a border collie. He's a Cardigan Welsh corgi. And he's blue merle." Belle informed her.

She set him on the floor. His short legs and long body had a comical look, especially when he tried to walk across the slick hardwood floor and his legs splayed in four directions.

Ruth studied the puppy. It looked so familiar, but she was pretty sure she'd never seen a corgi before. As she tried to remember where she'd seen such a dog, Jake dashed past the doorway. A moment later, he was back. He peeked his head into the door. "Oliver!" he yelled as he slid on his knees to the puppy. "You came!"

Ruth wrinkled her brow, "Do you know this puppy, Jake?"

Jake nodded with huge tosses of his head, "Kris told me."

"Do you know where he lives?"

He nodded again, "Cloud room." He picked up the puppy and hugged it against his chest. "Oliver!" he whispered into the pup's neck.

Ruth hadn't moved. She simply stared at Jake and the puppy. "I'll be right back," she said as she walked quickly into the dining room/cloud room. She turned on the ceiling light and stood back to look at the stains on the ceiling. Damned if that spot next to the kitchen door didn't look exactly like the puppy, even down to its mottled coat.

She stuck her head back into the living room. "Would you ladies mind coming in here for a few minutes? I want to show you something." They came as beckoned, then lined up next to Ruth, puzzled.

"What are we supposed to do?" Bea asked after a few silent seconds.

"Look at the stain next to the kitchen door," Ruth pointed. "What do you see?"

Sally was the first to respond. "I'll be damned. It's a corgi. A blue merle."

Ruth looked at Bea and Belle. They both nodded, eyes wide with amazement. "OK, thanks. I was afraid I'd gone 'round the bend. Let's go sit back down."

Jake was lying on his stomach, petting the puppy. Ruth sat on the floor next to him, "Jake, I'll watch the puppy. Will you go find your momma and ask her to come here?"

When he left, Ruth quickly related that Jake had told them that morning that he had dreamed he was getting a puppy named Oliver. "Then you turn up with one. By the way, what does *come by* mean?"

Belle looked at her with concern. "Turn right and circle clockwise. Why?"

"I don't know. I'm probably losing it. But both Bea and Sally called and asked if they could come by today. They said exactly the same words. It struck me as odd. Then I asked Sally and she said it was a herding term." She thought a second, "I don't know."

Belle looked interested, "A Cardigan is a herding dog."

"A what? I thought you said it was a corgi."

Belle nodded, "It is. There are two kinds of Welsh corgis – Pembroke and Cardigan, named for cities in Wales. Cardigans have tails; Pembrokes don't. This one is a Cardigan. They're both used for herding."

Janie walked into the room, followed by Jake. She greeted all the guests before noticing the puppy on Ruth's lap.

"Cute puppy," she said uncertainly. "Jake told me it came from Kris in the cloud room." She squinted at Ruth. "What the heck is going on?"

"I really don't know, Janie. Belle found the pup sitting on our sidewalk and thought it was ours. We'll figure it out. But right now would you take it so I can chat with my guests?"

Janie picked up the puppy. "We'll discuss this more later," she promised Ruth. "Come on, Jake. Let's take this puppy out on the porch."

"His name is Oliver, Momma."

The door to the porch slammed and quiet settled in. Ruth took a deep breath, "Sorry about this. I still don't know what's going on, but you didn't come over to get caught up in a puppy manifestation."

"I don't know," Belle smiled. "I think I may have precipitated it."

"One final question about the dog: does any of you know where the puppy might belong?" Ruth asked hopefully.

They shook their heads. Sally summed it up, "It doesn't belong around here. Nobody has ever had corgis."

"OK, then. So why did you all want to come by here today?"

Sally held up a hand, "Me first. My news also concerns Bea. Then we'll leave you and Bea to chat."

"Not necessary," Bea corrected. "I was going to come see you two later. If you stay, you'll save me a trip."

Ruth looked at each of them. "Would someone just tell me something? Anything."

Belle spoke up quickly. "Ruth, every year BellWhether Kennels sponsors a fundraiser for the county humane society. We hold it on our grounds. We've done things like a dog wash, a silent auction, a Dog Days dinner of hotdogs fixed every way conceivable. One of us has always run it. But it gets harder each year for us to carve off the time."

Sally chimed in, "We thought you did such a bang-up job on Janie's party, we wondered if you'd consider taking the lead on the benefit. It's wide open. You could do anything you want. BellWhether will foot the bill for expenses as long as it's not exorbitant. What do you say?"

"What a great idea," Bea added.

Ruth looked rather dazed overlaid with pleasure. "I think I'd like that, if I can count on you three for help and support." She looked at each nodding head, "OK. I'll do it!"

Sally threw her arms up in the air, "YAY! Oh, and I forgot to tell you that the benefit's usually the third weekend in October. It'll be cooler by then."

Ruth's smile grew even wider, "Thank you for asking me."

"Now it's my turn," Bea announced. She opened a large envelope she'd brought with her and extracted a photograph. She held it on her lap and looked at it for a long beat before speaking. "I went back to Arkansas to see if I could find my sister. I haven't spoken to her in over thirty years. I thought it was time."

She raised the photo from her lap and looked at it again. "Ruth," she said handing her the photo, "I don't know if you remember my sister, Ellen. She's six years younger than I am, just a kid when we were in high school." Ruth shook her head. "No, I didn't think so." Bea handed the photograph to Ruth. "As you can see, I found her. This was taken last week."

In the photo, Bea stood next to a slimmer but tireder-looking version of herself. "She really looks like you," Ruth declared as she passed the photo to Sally and Belle, sitting opposite her.

"Yes, she does," Bea agreed. "That was part of the problem." Sally and Belle looked at the photo carefully before handing it back to Ruth.

"I was married for three years to Larry Sprague. Do you remember him, Ruth? A year older than me. Football player — star quarterback. He went off to Viet Nam straight out of high school. Seemed to have been unaffected by it. Until he started drinking too much. And flirting with Ellen.

"He was such a handsome lout. Ellen was angry at me for leaving her at home to take care of Daddy after Mother got sick. She tried to sabotage me more than once. I had a miscarriage. Tried to eat away my unhappiness, gained a lot of weight, and lost interest in my 'wifely duties,' as my mother used to say.

"Ellen stepped right in. I caught them in bed together. That very night, I went to Daddy to borrow some money. I told him I had to leave before I killed someone. I don't think he was surprised. He said I could have part of my inheritance early. So I headed west, taking any road that caught my eye. I had no destination in mind; I just wanted to be away from Conway, Arkansas.

"Somehow I ended up in Edith and saw the diner for sale. I bought it with Daddy's money. And I never went back. I didn't go to Mother's or Daddy's funerals. I've never corresponded with Larry except to sign the divorce papers, and I've never had anything to do with Ellen.

"And then you showed up here," she patted Ruth's arm, "and that got me thinking. I'd been planning a trip back to Arkansas to see what relatives I had left — why not look for Ellen, too?

"Anyway, I found her living up in Springdale. She never married Larry. Never married at all. Worked with battered women for a while. Even ran the shelter. Now she's waiting tables at a greasy spoon. I think I'm going to offer her a job."

Ruth's mind raced. All she could think of were the reasons that was such a bad idea. Luckily her internal editor was keeping her mouth clamped shut. She said nothing. Only nodded.

Sally and Belle exchanged one of their looks. Then Sally suggested, "What if we offered her a job? Let you two get to know each other better before you commit."

"We've got a vacant apartment above the old kennel building. It would need some fixing up. But we could include its rent as part of her pay," Belle proposed.

A tear slid down Bea's cheek. "I wasn't expecting that. You don't even know her."

"No, and you don't either. We've got no history with her. We can fire her if need be. You can't fire a sister. Besides, we've all screwed up our lives in some way or another. And gotten a little help changing directions." Sally's voice was flat, matter-of-fact.

"But what would you want her to do? I don't even know what she *can* do." Bea looked from one concerned face to the other.

"Bea, we need all kinds of help – from receptionist to conference planning to kennel help to housekeeping. I think we can find something that would suit us all." Sally's confident tone eased Bea's worries.

"She could help me with the benefit," Ruth offered.

"Thank you all," Bea said quietly. "You offered me a real solution. I'll talk with Ellen and let you know." Bea stood up. "Now I've got to go to work." She hugged each of them before leaving.

"I am delighted you came up with that idea for Ellen. I couldn't see anything but problems if Bea hired her right now, but I had nothing to offer Bea instead. Your suggestion was both brilliant and very kind." Ruth hugged them both as they prepared to leave.

"One last thing, Belle. Why would you ever tell a dog to turn right and circle clockwise? I can't imagine ever needing that command."

"You would if you were trying to gather up your flock," Belle's smile faded to wry glance. "Like Bea is."

After her visitors left, Ruth found Janie, Jake, and Oliver on the back porch. "I don't know what we should do about this puppy," she said. "Should we put up FOUND posters and see if anyone responds?"

Janie agreed, "I already called the vet. He said he'd never seen a corgi in his practice." She handed a flat bowl to Jake. "Hon, would you go get the puppy some water?"

"Oliver, Momma."

"OK. Get Oliver some water." When Jake had got out of ear-shot, Janie leaned forward and said quietly, "I hope nobody claims this dog. It would break Jake's heart."

"I know. But are you okay with getting a dog now?"

Janie shrugged. "I had planned to get him a dog this fall, after it cools down, so that he can go outside and play more. But Oliver happened. And he's a great puppy. He even comes when Jake calls him."

"But it's worrisome – the way he showed up after Jake's dream. Very big coincidence."

"Maybe it's not a coincidence. Maybe it's magic," Janie replied solemnly.

Eleven

"Never repeat yourself unless you're instructing a parrot."
Velma Lee Lewis

Lying on the breakfast table at his mother's place was a hand-written journal Bradley had found at work. He was pleased with himself. He knew that his mother would like it. In fact, many people would probably like it. He'd been careful to check with Seth before he took it from the house, but Seth assured him there were no heirs except the county, and the county had given explicit instructions that all the remaining contents were to be considered trash.

It was just luck that he even found it. He was cleaning out a closet when the book fell off an upper shelf and landed on his foot. He initially threw it into the trash heap where he'd been sweeping all the dust bunnies and mouse turds, but he had second thoughts. He picked it up and stuck it in his pocket to examine later.

That had been yesterday. He forgot about it until he'd undressed last night for bed. Then he'd sat up late reading through it. Of course, he knew some of it – what person from Plainview or Edith didn't – but new bits caught him off guard and made him laugh. He chuckled again thinking of it.

Hal ambled into the kitchen and poured himself some coffee. Bradley had been so busy since Hal came home he'd barely had time to speak to him. First he helped Seth on the clean-up of Bea Murphy's place, then Seth asked him to work with him on the renovation of a once grand house that had belonged to Miss Velma Lee Lewis. Thus the journal.

"Hey, BB," Hal mumbled. It still surprised him to see how grown-up his little brother had gotten. Off to college in a few weeks. He'd do fine. He was the most hard-working, conscientious person Hal had ever known. He could hardly believe they were brothers.

"Hey. You're up early," Bradley commented. "Got big plans today?"

"Mmm. Kind of. Gotta get my car cleaned up and checked out. Taking Gerry Krane over to Buffalo for dinner tonight. What's the name of that place Mom went the other day? Didn't she say it was pretty good?" Hal finished one cup of coffee before leaving the counter.

"I don't know how you do that," Bradley said, staring.

"Do what?"

"Drink hot coffee that fast. Doesn't it burn?"

With a shrug, Hal dismissed the question. "So what's the name of that place in Buffalo?"

"Dunno. Ask Mom." Bradley mumbled through a mouthful of cereal.

"Ask Mom what?" Betsy King stepped briskly into the kitchen dressed for work in slacks and a linen tunic.

"The name of that new restaurant in Buffalo. I'm taking Gerry Krane there tonight."

Betsy stopped pouring cereal into her bowl and looked at her son, "Is that a good idea?"

"I don't know if it's a good idea or not, but what's the name of the damned restaurant?" Hal's voice rose in pitch and volume.

"Dizzy's. And watch your mouth with me. I'm still your mother." She poured the milk, and slammed the carton back into the fridge.

"Yes, ma'm." Hal carried his cup out the door. "Later," he mumbled a few seconds before his car door slammed and his motor roared into life.

"Damn! Why can't I just keep my mouth shut?" Betsy asked.

"Same reason he can't, I guess." Bradley just wanted a quiet meal and to surprise his mother. Hal always injected too much drama.

Betsy patted Bradley's head as she walked past. She set her bowl on her placemat and noticed the book lying beside it. "What's this?"

"Something I found at work. I thought you might like it."

Bradley's diffident grin always made Betsy proud. She smiled at him before opening the cover of the book. When she saw the name written of the top of the first page – Velma Lee Lewis – her eyes widened, her eyebrows rose, and a smile spread slowly across her face.

The first entry in the book was from 1927. She laughed as she read it aloud to Bradley, "Rouge on the knees is a wasted effort. It draws no attention and stains petticoats."

She flipped several pages, "Oh my God, BB! This is wonderful! I can't wait to go through it all. But, unfortunately, I have to go to work. Thank you, baby!" She kissed his cheek before gathering her bags and keys. "Bye. Have a good day. And thanks again!"

Bradley happily ate his breakfast before pedaling his bicycle off to Miss Velma Lee's house. He had made enough money working with Seth to pay for his school expenses. Now he was working on a car. And who knew, he might find another treasure today.

Sitting at the end of the road and watching for his mother to drive by, Hal felt like a bratty child. Why did he have to cause a fuss every time his mother showed any negative reaction to him? Hell, this time she was probably worried about him getting hurt – he'd moped around for months when he'd broken off with Gerry five years ago. He watched Betsy drive by and was torn about whether to drive after her and apologize or go back to the house for breakfast, now that the coast was clear.

His stomach won. He saw BB ride off on his bike, then pulled back into the driveway and parked in the carport. He'd have the morning to himself. He could eat in peace and work on the song he wanted to write for Gerry.

He sat at the table with another cup of coffee and a bowl of cereal and milk. An old book at his mother's place caught his eye.

He picked it up and idly leafed through it until he nearly spit his coffee with an explosion of laughter as he read, "Boys in short pants should wear tight underwear."

He flipped back to the beginning of the book and confirmed that it had, indeed, belonged to Miss Velma Lee. "What a windfall! These are too good," he said to himself. "I've got to find a way to use this." He carried the book off to his room, forgetting the bowl of cereal he hadn't yet touched.

He picked up his guitar and strummed a few chords. Could he use some of the sayin's in a song? He could almost hear the melody. He strummed another three chords, humming along with them. That was it, that melancholy sound. Now if he could just find a few sayin's to pull into the lyrics, he might have a good apology for his mother.

Three and a half hours later, Hal still sat on his bed, copying sayin's onto a pad of paper and humming a tune. He glanced at the clock and jumped straight up. He had accomplished none of the things he had set out to do. But he was so close. He looked at the clock again. He could work a little more. He almost had the rhythm and tune working with the sayin's he'd selected.

By the time he had all the lyrics written, he knew he had to hustle to be ready for his date with Gerry. But he sang through them once more. He was pleased with the song. He thought it was reminiscent of The Beatles' "Eleanor Rigby."

Velma Lee Lewis lived in a house all alone
in the middle of town.
Nobody knew her, they guessed who she was
from the things she wrote down.
And she wrote them all down —
All the rules she'd invented,
All the manners she taught,
So that she and her image
Would be seen as they ought.

They called them her sayin's, the rules she believed
that would keep her from harm.

She taught all the children to sit, speak, and eat
    with good manners and charm.
Oh, she wrote them all down—
    All the rules she'd invented,
    All the manners she taught,
    So her etiquette students
    would behave as they ought.

"Never eat onions after the first of July"
        and "Wait until May
to polish the silver" and "Dust all the books
        on a bright sunny day."
Oh, she wrote them all down—
    All the rules she'd invented,
    All the manners she taught,
    'Til she died old and lonely
    and her rules came to naught.

Hal carried the book back to his mother's place at the table. He'd sing her the song when he saw her. Right now, he needed to tend to his car.

Bea waited until the last lunch customers had left the diner before placing a call to her sister. "Ellen, it's Jo," she announced when Ellen answered. She'd decided she wanted to be Jo again. She would start working on converting her friends right away.

"Hey, Jo. What's up?"

For a minute, Bea froze. She didn't know what to say that didn't sound condescending. "I've got something I want to discuss with you. Do you have a few minutes?"

"I guess. Sure." Ellen's tone betrayed her nervousness. She wasn't yet certain that she could trust her sister. After all, she'd done a horrible thing. How could Jo forgive her? She didn't think she could have forgiven if the roles were reversed. Which, thank God, they weren't.

"I was wondering if you, er, um, I have some friends who own a large kennel. They are always looking for good help. They also have an apartment for rent. I know you're working and have friends in Springdale, but I wondered if you would consider moving here and working for my friends. It would let us really get to know each other again." Bea finished her speech in a rush.

"Why, Jo, that's an interesting idea if I were thinking about moving which I might be since I've only lived here for about six months and my boyfriend who I moved here with has left."

Bea swallowed hard, "Um, would you like to come over and see the place? Meet my friends? Look at the apartment? Talk to them about a job?" Bea couldn't seem to slow herself down.

Ellen didn't seem to notice, "I could probably come over there next week since I have to work every day but Thursday this week and I think it's too far for me to drive, but I don't know how far it is."

Bea hesitated. Had Ellen asked a question? "What?"

"Well I need to know how far it is so I can plan when I could come and make sure I don't miss too much work in case things don't work out and I have to come back here."

"It's about six hours."

"Then this week won't work since I only have Thursday off and six hours twice is more than I want to drive in one day even if I had a place to stay which I'll need the next week on Tuesday if that's OK."

"So you can come a week from Tuesday?" Bea was feeling word-battered. She hadn't noticed Ellen's talking so much when she was with her.

"Yes, I can leave on Tuesday morning next week, not this week, and get there in the early afternoon when I can talk to your friends and see the place then I can stay over until the next morning and be back here in time to take care of my laundry and things before I have to go to work on Thursday, not this Thursday when I'm off but next Thursday."

"Um, OK. Um, let me call my friends to see it that works for them. I'll call you back."

"If I don't answer it's probably because I'm either working or taking a shower since I don't take my phone with me either of those places or I'd likely get fired, well, not in the shower."

"I'll leave a message," Bea said quickly, "Bye, now."

"Bye, Jo. I'm really glad you called because I'm not all that crazy about this town – there are too many cars and chickens around here."

Bea really didn't want to hear about the chickens. "Bye," she said and hung up the phone. She put her head in her hands and cried out, "Oh, my God! What was I thinking?" No one in the empty diner replied.

After a piece of her own favorite pumpkin pie and a cup of tea, Bea had calmed down and called BellWhether. As the phone rang, she wished she smoked. At least she could calm down without getting fat. But there was lung cancer. Dear God, she was starting to sound like Ellen.

Sally answered with a gruff, "BellWhether Kennels."

"Is this a bad time, Sal? I can call you back."

"No, it's fine. I'm just hoarse from calling to a puppy who decided to go walkabout."

"If you catch him, name him Boomerang."

"Funny. I might. So what's going on with you?" Sally's good humor had returned.

"Well, first off, I called Ellen. She can be here a week from Tuesday. Will that work for you?"

"I think so. Hold on," she took the phone away from her ear and asked Belle who was sitting at her desk if she had any plans for that day. After getting a head-shake, Sally picked the phone back up. "That will be fine. I'll put it on the calendar. Morning or afternoon?"

"Afternoon. She's going to drive over that day."

"Got it. Anything else?"

Bea took a deep breath. "I want you to promise me that if you don't think it will work, you won't hire her. OK?"

"OK. You sound worried."

"I guess I am," Bea admitted. "When I spoke to her today she blathered so much that I barely knew what she said. It was really off-putting. If she does that all the time, you won't be able to stand having her around. So promise me, you won't just hire her to please me."

"OK. I promise. But she was probably just nervous."

"She'll be nervous meeting you and Belle, too."

Sally's calm voice reassured Bea, "Then I guess we'll see how she is when she gets here. Don't worry. It'll all work out somehow."

"Thanks, Sal. One last thing. Do you think you could learn to call me Jo?"

Sally chuckled, "I expect I could. Just don't get upset if I forget sometimes. Old dogs and new tricks, you know."

"Horse feathers! You teach old dogs new tricks day in and day out. Ask Belle for me, too, would you?"

"Sure will, Bea, er, Jo."

"See, that wasn't so hard! Thanks again, Sally. Talk with you soon."

Bea liked being called Jo again. Jo wouldn't be so indecisive about calling Ellen back. OK, dammit, she'd do it right now.

When Ellen answered, Bea told her quickly that the dates would work. "Plan to spend the night at my house. I've got plenty of room." Now why did she say that? She didn't want Ellen to think she could move in with her.

"OK, Jo. Thanks again for arranging this so that I don't have to miss too much work and have a place to stay where I don't have to pay a motel bill since the gas will cost a lot as it is."

"See you next week, Ellen," Bea hung up quickly. She just couldn't listen any more.

The two sets of pages were ready to take with her to Bell-Whether. Gerry only needed to call and confirm that Belle was available for a story-telling session. She needed the tale of how they happened to move from Dodge City to Plainview.

After a quick call, Gerry gathered up the pages into folders and drove to the kennel. Belle was waiting for her in the office. "Hi, Belle. Thanks for taking time to do this."

"It's really pretty quiet right now. I'll enjoy rocking on the porch with a glass of iced tea." Belle led the way back to the porch.

Gerry added lemon to her tea, "Before I forget, I brought you each a draft of the Dusty story. It's ready for you to read and correct." She handed the folders to Belle. "I was surprised how quickly the writing went. I hope I have all the facts straight."

"We'll read it tonight. You write so well, it will be a real pleasure."

"Thanks, Belle. I hope I did okay with that story. I want the tension to build to the end."

"It was tense, all right." Belle leaned back in her rocker and began to tell the story of Sally's recovery from the shooting.

About an hour later, Gerry left with many more notes and a new appreciation of the accomplishment these two wounded women had achieved in building BellWhether Kennels.

Hal's car was so clean he almost didn't recognize it in the grocery store parking lot. He wanted to take a little gift to Gerry, but he couldn't think of what it should be. He wandered the aisles of the store to see if anything jumped out at him.

He was about to give up when he came to the Specialty Foods shelf and found a jar of ginger marmalade. He bought it. He really hoped that Gerry still liked ginger. He had called her Ginger for a while. Her red hair reminded him of the sultry beauty on "Gilligan's Island." The reference was lost on her. She'd never seen the show.

His mother was crazy about Gilligan. Somewhere she'd gotten videotapes of about two dozen episodes. He'd seen them all, many times. Maybe he'd show a few to Gerry sometime.

He'd dressed carefully in new jeans, a bright blue polo shirt, and boots. He knew the blue of the shirt intensified the color of his eyes. Gerry knew it, too. She'd given him the shirt. After they broke up, he couldn't bear to wear it.

Gerry and Jessie were playing Frisbee when Hal drove up. She'd done it on purpose – he didn't need to guess how nervous she was or how much time she'd spent getting ready. "Hi!" she greeted him, looking him up and down with exaggerated head turns. "You look nice. Would you throw the Frisbee to Jess a couple more times while I go get my things?"

He took the Frisbee and threw a pop-up that Jess leaped to catch. "Great catch, Jessie," he praised her. The second toss was more direct – straight at her. Jess lazily turned her head a fraction of an inch and plucked the Frisbee out of the air as if it were nothing. Hal pounded her sides. "You are the coolest dog!" he told her.

Gerry, at the door, called Jess in. She told her to behave and watch the house, a ritual they always performed when Gerry left Jess at home. Jess lay down on the throw rug by the door where she could look through the sidelight and watch Gerry walk down the walk toward Hal.

When they got in the car, he presented her with a brown paper bag. "For you," he said and kissed her cheek.

She opened the bag and looked at Hal in surprise as she removed the jar of marmalade. "I can't believe you remembered how much I like this stuff. Thank you!" She returned the cheek kiss.

Hal leaned back against his very recently cleaned seat. This is going pretty fine, he told himself. The song ought to seal the deal.

She was saying something that he missed. "Sorry. Daydreaming. What did you say?"

"I said, 'Aren't you going to start the car?' Hello!"

An abashed Hal started the car and drove silently down the street. She patted him on the thigh, "It's good to see you again, Hal."

She must be feeling good about him, he decided. She had rarely called him anything but Prince.

After a good-enough dinner and pleasant conversation, Hal drove them back to Gerry's house. "May I come in for a little while?" he asked as he opened the car door for her.

"Sure. Want a night cap?"

"Maybe just a cup of coffee," Hal answered as he opened the trunk and got out his guitar.

Gerry looked at it with a frown, but led the way into her kitchen nonetheless. She made coffee and took Jessie out for a quick game of catch while Hal tuned and picked his guitar.

When the coffee was brewed, she poured each of them a cup and pulled out a bottle of Bailey's Irish Cream. A splash in each cup gave the coffee a rich aroma. She lifted the cup to her nose as she sat across from Hal.

He drank nearly half of the cup of steaming coffee before saying, "I wrote something for my mother today, but I thought you might like to hear it, too. Actually, my mother hasn't even heard it yet."

Gerry leaned back in her chair to listen. Hal had a nice voice, she remembered. He played an introduction that reminded her of something – something sad and haunting in a minor key.

When he began to sing, she was charmed. She knew his mother would love the song, as would Janie. He repeated the final chorus in almost a whisper:

> *All the rules she'd invented,*
> *All the manners she taught,*
> *'Til she died old and lonely*
> *and her rules came to naught.*

"Oh, Prince! That was wonderful! Whatever made you write about Miss Velma Lee?"

"BB found her hand-written journal when he was helping with the restoration of her old house. He brought it home to Mom."

"Oh, I really want to see that journal! Do you think your mother would lend it to me?" Gerry's cheeks flushed in excitement.

"Probably, but why?"

"I think I have to write about her – Miss Velma Lee. I don't know why, but I feel it very strongly." Gerry's excitement was growing. She nearly shook with it.

"Aren't you already writing a book?" Hal asked.

"Yes, but I'm nearly finished with it. And then Janie's aunt, Ruth Welborne, wants me to work on a project with her to publish her travel experiences as a memoir or a fictionalized account. But that would be mostly an editing job. They're her stories."

"Wouldn't Miss Velma Lee's stories be *her* stories?"

"Not in the same way, I don't think. I'll have to see her journal first before I decide. Could I look at it soon? This weekend?"

"I'll ask Mom tomorrow and let you know. That really jazzes you, huh?"

"Yeah, it does. It's what I want to do. Write."

"I get that. I lost track of everything this morning when I was working on my song." His smile was so genuine that Gerry had to hold herself back.

"Hal, I need to say good night. I have to work on the story that Belle Sheppard told me this afternoon. I need to get it down while it's still fresh." She stood up and took his hand. "Thank you for a wonderful evening. But most of all, thank you for sharing your song." She kissed his cheek.

He tried to turn his head for a more satisfying kiss, but Gerry stepped back. He brushed her jaw with the backs of his fingers. "Goodnight, Ger. I'll call you tomorrow after I talk to Mom."

She walked him to the door and waved as he drove away. She heaved a sigh and sat down at her laptop to write Belle's story. Funny that she just now realized how much she wanted to write a story of her own.

BellWhether Tails

BellWhether's Nothin' But Blue Skyes – 1984

Things were crazy after Sally got shot. She was in and out of the hospital. Multiple surgeries. Rehabilitation treatments and physical therapy. Months of doctors, hospitals, and even more doctors.

When she was home, Dusty was pasted to her side. He even slept with her. The only dog who slept in the house. But he'd earned it.

Sally was determined to go back to work and nearly killed herself trying. She exercised her knee until she nearly dropped from exhaustion. But the mobility didn't return. The knee was too damaged. All the king's horses and all the king's men....

About the time Sally was coming to terms with the permanence of her injury, a puppy buyer from Memphis accidentally left a copy of the *Commercial Appeal* on my desk. I absently picked it up and flipped through it. A small article in the middle of the first section caught my eye. I read it twice before it sunk in. And then I dropped it on the floor in absolute shock. Johnny Benton had been released from the West Tennessee State Penitentiary.

I flew into a panic. I had to leave Dodge City. I had to hide. Again. But I could do neither. Sally needed me.

I walked around like a zombie. I thought I was hiding my emotional state from Sally, even though I was up in the middle of every night pacing, packing, planning and panicking.

After a couple weeks of this behavior, Sally confronted me, "Bell, what's going on? You look like hell; you're losing weight; your hands shake. I know you're worn out from tending me. Let's hire some help. You need to rest. Get away from me and the dogs for a while."

"No!" I fired back. "I'm not going anywhere. I took a leave to be here for you. I'm going to damned well *be* here."

"Bell. Talk to me."

I felt tears fill my eyes. I don't cry. I wouldn't now. I swiped them away impatiently with the back of my hand. "It's not you. It's me. My past. Coming after me." I hugged myself tightly.

Sally watched with concern. "What in your past?"

"Oh, Sally. It's an old sordid story. You don't want to hear it."

Sally's hand smoothed Dusty's head. He had moved to her side when he sensed her upset. "Talk to me, Bell. Let me help if I can."

All of my instincts flashed "RUN" in bright red lights. I ignored them. It was time to talk. "Remember when I first came to Dodge City in 1960? I told you I needed to legally change my name because of a divorce. That was a lie."

"OK."

"I'm not divorced. I needed to change my name to hide. From him. From Johnny."

Sally nodded.

"My real name is Julia Edith Campbell Smith Benton. Born Campbell, adopted as Smith, married to Benton. Johnny Benton."

Sally absently smoothed Dusty's ears and waited.

"Johnny hit me. Beat me. I had a child. Mary Nell. When she was just two, he threatened to hurt her. I sent her off to my Aunt Bess Campbell in Kansas City. Johnny nearly killed me over that. When I could travel, I left. Wound up here. Changed my name. Hid."

I saw sympathy in Sally's face, but she said nothing.

"Johnny went to prison. He just got out. He'll come for me. I have to leave. I can't let him find me. Or you."

I paced as I spoke. Sally watched for several minutes. "Bell, sit down. I've got the beginnings of an idea. Let me think a minute." She closed her eyes and smoothed Dusty's head. She took a breath and looked up, "OK. This is still rough but just listen.

"I'm not going to be a deputy any more. My knee is never going to be normal. I've been pretending to myself that everything could go back the way it was, but it won't. It can't.

"I can be pensioned off on disability. I don't know the amount, but it will be substantial. I've been with the department for damned near thirty years!"

I felt some of my fear recede.

"What if we relocated? Instead of building a bigger kennel and expanding our business here, what if we went somewhere else? I could go there as myself. I've got some name recognition in bloodhounds. You could come with a new name."

"And my dogs?"

"I don't know. I mean, you could bring them, of course. But I don't know how to let them be who they are. Champions aren't anonymous."

I pushed my hair off my forehead as I thought. "What if I didn't tout them? Started over with younger dogs? Brought in some new blood?"

"That might work."

"What if we came up with a new kennel name? Registered all the new dogs with it? My older dogs wouldn't be immediately evident in the pedigree. If anybody asked, I'd say I got the dogs from a woman who closed her business." I managed to smile as I said it.

Sally raised an eyebrow, "Yeah. That might work. Maybe we could find a kennel to buy. Somebody wanting to retire."

"Let's look. I've got a little time. He won't find me for a few weeks. It's a cold trail, and I used diversions."

"Even Dusty might have trouble with that," Sally grinned as she continued to pat and smooth his head and ears. "I'll call Jo Beth. Maybe she knows somebody."

Later that day, Sally started working on her disability pension. She said she thought the sheriff was relieved. He didn't want to be the one to have to tell her she couldn't come back.

She called Jo Beth, followed leads, and came up with two possibilities. "I'll call and talk to the owners. Can you do some research on their locations? Go see if they're in areas where we'd like to live?" She handed me a sheet with kennel names and cities scrawled in her distinctive writing.

The first was just outside Jackson, Tennessee. I vetoed that immediately. Too close to Memphis. And Johnny.

The second was in Oklahoma. Plainview. I'd never heard of it. I'd been to Plainview, Texas, for a herding trial but had spent little time in Oklahoma. Only Tulsa and Oklahoma City. I went to the library and spent a couple of hours researching.

That evening I told Sally I thought we could live in Plainview. "It's in northwest Oklahoma, not near much of anything. I like the idea of hiding out in Plainview," I grinned.

She looked blank for a beat, then rolled her eyes. "Ha. Yeah." She described what she'd found out. "Sixty acres attached with the kennel. Enough for expansion, herding fields, and trailing courses. The kennel building is attached to the house by a covered walkway – good for winter. Kennel has twenty-five runs. Everything is usable but needs work, he said."

"Why's he want to sell?"

"His wife died. He's getting old – seventy-eight. His daughter wants him to move to Enid, near her."

"Dogs?"

"He's sold off most everything. Has only a couple left and wants to keep them. He might sell me one, a top-twenty trailer from Jo Beth's line. Name of Duke. I'd like to use him with Daisy."

"Make little Hazards?" Another big eye-roll from Sally. "Maybe he'd let you breed to Duke even if he doesn't sell him."

"Maybe. Anyway, I think it's worth a look-see."

"When?"

"Next weekend? I can clear all my medical appointments for Friday and Monday. OK?"

"OK." I nodded with more enthusiasm than I felt. I didn't want to go to Plainview as Edie Bell.

The next day, a trip to the drugstore helped me implement my first step in becoming someone else. I'd been coloring my hair for a few years to cover the "premature" gray. I bought a color stripper. By evening I'd aged a few years.

I dug out my old glasses and put away the contacts. Not a drastic change, but I hoped enough to keep me from being immediately identified. Besides, I'd learned over the years, nobody really looks at middle-aged women.

As I got ready for our trip to Plainview, now gray-haired and bespectacled, I felt another edge of fear crumble away.

We made the trip to Plainview. The kennel, house, and land would work. We made an offer.

A couple of weeks later, Sally reviewed the counter-offer with the realtor over the phone. When she hung up she demanded, "We need names."

"For what?"

"You and the kennel."

"Oh, yeah. I've been working on it. Do you like Ann or Jane better?"

"I don't really care. I'm going to keep calling you 'Bell' whether that's your name or not."

I snorted in disgust. Bell! Then a light clicked on. "*B-e-l-l-e* is a first name."

"Um-hmm."

"I could be *B-e-l-l-e*, Belle, rather than *B-e-l-l*, Bell."

"OK."

"Tell me again what you said you'd call me."

Sally looked at me askance, but complied, "I said I'd call you 'Bell' whether that was your name or not."

"Bell whether. Bellwether. BellWhether. How about Bell-Whether for a kennel name – Bell with one e and Whether with two *h*'s. Too cute?"

"No. I like it. You can still be Bell, with a silent e." She grinned, "Or would you rather be 'Belly'?"

My turn to roll my eyes. "Funny."

"Last name?"

"I don't know. Something doggy – cocker? No. Shepherd?"

"Not bad. *S-h-e-p-h-e-r-d?*"

"More subtle. *S-h-e-p-p-a-r-d?*"

"Belle Sheppard? I like it." Sally nodded approval.

I repeated it to myself several times. "Yeah. I do, too."

"Then you need to get it legalized fast. We need to sign the papers on the kennel in two weeks."

I'd already resigned from my job. It was just a formality. I'd been on leave since Sally was shot. They'd even replaced me. "My final paycheck from the sheriff's office is due tomorrow. I'll deposit it and clean out the account. Then get my name legally changed next week. Goodbye Edie Bell."

"Sad about it?"

"No, not now. I chose it when I was running away. Now I'm running to."

That night Sally said, "I'm ordering business cards and letterhead for our new kennel tomorrow. Last chance to change the name."

"I'm satisfied. Bell-Whether just goes with Plain-view, don't you think?"

"Done. BellWhether Kennels of Plainview, Oklahoma. Here we come."

That night, for the first time in weeks, I slept with un-clenched teeth.

I hadn't told Sally that I'd been in contact with Emma Campbell in Dunvegan, Isle of Skye, Scotland, again. I wanted a breeding age dog and a young bitch to breed to my existing dogs to create a new BellWhether line. The day the letter with the flight arrangements came was the first time Sally had heard of my plan. My excitement spread to her. We could hardly wait for the first litter.

I made a whirlwind trip to pick up the dogs. I wasn't dis-appointed. The male was white and a gorgeous dilute black — that dark gray color called "blue." His name, Blue, was easy. The young bitch was about eleven months old. Black and white with tip ears and a wonderful set of shoulders. I called her Tipper.

Within a week of their arrival, Bramble, one of my four-year-old bitches went into heat. Fourteen days from then would be one of our first days in Plainview. I'd breed Bramble to Blue in our new kennel.

When I told Sally of my plans, "Better think up some good names," was her smiling reply.

We got moved. I had a new name. Sally sold the ranch to Doug McAllister, our kennel helper. He'd bought a coup-le of my border collies and one of Sally's bloodhounds. He said he preferred herding, but he figured with Sally gone he could hire out to the sheriff's office with the bloodhound.

We met some of the local people in Plainview. We par-ticularly liked the woman who ran the Edith Diner. She looked like Andy Taylor's Aunt Bea. Sally called her Bea ac-cidentally. She loved it. Laughed 'til the tears streamed down her cheeks.

Bramble was due in the next few days. It only takes nine weeks to cook new puppies. Women are always en-vious. But it seems a long time when you're waiting.

Bramble told us when she was ready. Not one to suffer in silence, she yipped, whimpered, and whined throughout her problem-free deliveries. I had decided to keep the first-born regardless of sex, but I was particularly pleased with the pretty little blue bitch who initiated our new kennel. I named her BellWhether's Nothin' but Blue Skyes – Skye – and prayed it was an accurate forecast.

Twelve

"Never tell your friends what you wear to bed."
Velma Lee Lewis

The fort was complete. Or complete enough. Win had spent nearly two hours with Jake, Oliver, and a stack of scrap wood. At the end of the session the fort was secure. Its four-foot-tall walls surrounded an open square area of ten feet on a side. In the middle was the "block house" in fort lingo. Win told Jake it could be his headquarters and Oliver it could be his outdoor shelter. Both approved.

As did Janie. She watched Win with Jake and Win with Oliver. For a man with no experience with a boy or a dog, he was amazing. He teased, taught, and tussled with Jake, keeping an eye on Oliver while he did.

It was Win's idea to put a doghouse in the center of Jake's fort. Since nobody had any information about Oliver, he assumed that the dog was there to stay. He built a boy-sized door in one side and a dog-sized one in another. Jake wanted to sleep in it with Oliver. Janie was less than excited by that idea. But when Win came over after dinner with two air mattresses and sleeping bags, Janie conceded.

"You're really going to sleep out there in that 'fort' with Jake and Oliver?" Janie looked up at him in disbelief.

"Well, sure." Win shrugged his right shoulder in dismissal.

"In this heat?"

"I'll bring a fan."

"Why would you do that?" Janie was truly puzzled. It seemed not to be anything a sane person would undertake.

"Because you only get to spend the first night in your new fort once," he said seriously. "When you're four, first moments matter."

She kissed his cheek on tiptoe. "They matter when you're twenty-seven, too," she whispered in his ear.

Win thought the look in Janie's eyes was worth a night of heat and bugs.

Ruth looked out the back window as soon as she got up the next morning. She wanted to see how Win, Jake, and Oliver had fared. Honestly, she was surprised they hadn't come in during the night. Jake must have tried hard to impress Win with his bravery.

She couldn't see Jake's head, but his body was half in and half out of the doghouse. Oliver lay outside the building between Jake's legs and Win's back. She reached for her camera. This would be a great Facebook posting. Maybe she'd write a bit, too. Describe Plainview and their gentle giant neighbor.

She composed a few sentences in her head while she made coffee then grabbed a pen and the grocery list pad to write them down while the coffee brewed.

And she kept writing. About coming to Plainview with Janie and Jake, finding an old friend, and discovering new interests in this unlikely place.

When she quit to pour her coffee, she had filled the entire pad. She read through what she'd written and thought it wasn't too bad. Maybe she'd show it to Gerry. She didn't know what she'd do with it – it was too long for Facebook – but it felt good to write it. Maybe she'd email it to some of her old colleagues, although she didn't think they'd much care about her current simple pleasures.

While she considered what insight that gave her, Janie sat down beside her. "All the boys still asleep?" she asked, looking at the window.

"I think so. I haven't checked for a while."

"What have you been doing?" Janie noticed that Ruth was reading through the grocery list pad. "Find something interesting in the grocery list? Some intrigue? Are the bananas running around with the peaches?"

"Funny," Ruth rolled her eyes. "No, I used it to write down a few thoughts. I seem to have gotten carried away." She flipped through the pad. "I used it all."

"Oh, no! Whatever shall we do? We can't go to the grocery store again!" Janie threw her hands up with high melodrama. Ruth's scowl knocked her down a notch. "Sorry. Can I see what you wrote?"

"Later. I don't think you could read my scribbles. Let me transcribe them first. I'll print you a copy." She left the table with the pad. "I'm going to work on it now."

After she left, Janie looked out the window. She could see Win stretching and Oliver scurrying to the doorway in which Jake was sprawled. A puppy pounce later, Jake crawled out into the morning sunshine.

Win sat up and said something to Jake, who nodded seriously before he crawled back inside the building and pulled out his air mattress and sleeping bag. Win showed him how to let the air out of the mattress and roll up the bag. Jake stacked them on the ground next to the gate before the two of them, tagged by Oliver, left the fort and walked to the back porch.

Janie threw open the door to greet them. Jake dashed inside a split-second before Oliver. Win brought up the rear, stretching his back by bending from side to side. His hair stuck up in peaks, his glasses were tilted at an odd angle, and his clothes were heavily wrinkled.

Jake danced from foot to foot, "Oh, Momma, it was so cool. We sleeped in the fort all night. And Oliver sleeped next to me and Mr. Mailman guarded. Can we do it again tonight?"

Win groaned, Janie grinned, and Oliver barked.

The phone woke Gerry. She reached for it and mumbled a greeting. Jessie bumped Gerry's elbow, mashing the phone into Gerry's lip. "Unh," she groaned.

"Gerry, this is Betsy King. Are you all right?"

Gerry sat up straight, "Oh, Mrs. King. Good morning. Yes, I'm fine." She tried to make her voice sound well-oiled, as if she'd been up for hours.

"Oh, I woke you. I'm sorry. I forget that not everyone gets up with the birds."

"No, no. It's fine."

"I'm calling because Prince Hal tells me you'd like to borrow the Velma Lee Lewis journal."

"Oh, yes, I would," Gerry's enthusiasm brightened her husky voice.

"I'd like to have a chance to look it over before I lend it to you. But I can do that today. You can borrow it tomorrow, if you'd like."

"Oh, that's wonderful. What time should I come get it?" She heard mumbled conversation from the phone. "I'm sorry. I didn't catch that."

"Sorry, Gerry. Prince Hal said he'd bring it over around 9:30 if you'd have the coffee on."

"Tell him I'll make a big pot. And thanks to you both."

She still felt groggy, but the news that she'd have the journal to look at the next day helped wake her up. She'd lain awake for hours last night thinking about what she'd like to write. She wasn't lacking in ideas. In fact, she had too many. She'd have to figure out how to narrow them down into something plausible.

She had to finish **BellWhether Tails** first before she got embroiled in something else. And she'd told Ruth that she'd work with her on the travel project. Damn! She had gone from nothing to do to too much in less than a week.

The best way to get past the over-commitment, she told herself, was to finish the BellWhether piece. She'd do that this morning – proof the latest story and take it to Belle and Sally for approval.

She worked quickly, finished proofing, got a shower, and got dressed in under an hour. Jessie had been patient, but Gerry had to walk her before she left. As she passed Janie and Ruth's house, Ruth called out, "Good morning, Gerry."

"Hey, Ruth. Nice morning, huh?" She walked across the yard to where Ruth sat on the porch steps.

"Surprisingly so. I came out for a little air and have stayed while I edited this." She waved a stack of papers in front of her.

"What's that? Are you working on your travel piece?"

"No, it's just a kind of reflection on moving here and what I've learned in the process."

"That sounds interesting."

"You know, I think it's pretty good. But I need an objective observer. Would you read it and tell me what you think?" She held the pages out to Gerry.

Gerry took the papers and sat on the porch step next to Ruth to read them.

A few minutes later, Gerry looked up with a smile. "I think you've just written your first blog entry."

"I don't really know what that means. I know what a blog is, but I've never read any. Why would I want to write one?"

"Do some research and then we'll talk about it. Here, hand me your pen and I'll write you a starter list. Go look them up, follow their links to others, and theirs to even more."

"OK. I will."

"And while you're doing that, think about using a blog for your travel memoirs. There are travel sites that host blogs."

"I'd been thinking about a book for my travel stuff," Ruth frowned.

"You can still do that. There are tools that let you turn a blog into a book."

"Oh, lord! There's so much to learn. I'll start looking at blogs today. Thanks, Gerry." She took the pages back and gave Gerry a one-armed hug. "If I did that, I wouldn't need you to write it for me. Would you mind that?"

Gerry shook her head. "No. Not at all. I'd love to see you do this yourself. And be my Proofing Pal."

"What's a Proofing Pal?"

"You proof mine, and I'll proof yours. It's so hard to see your own typos."

"I get it. And I like it. I'd love to be your Proofing Pal."

"Let me know when you're ready. I have five BellWhether stories ready for you. I'll have one more as soon as Sally and Belle approve it."

"Bring them on. I'm happy to do it. And maybe one day soon, I'll have something for you to proof for me."

"You already do. Give me back those pages and I'll do a proper proofing."

"Gerry, I am so glad I ran into you this morning."

"Me, too. I've got to go deliver the last story to Sally and Belle. But I'll print a copy of all of them and bring them by later. See you then." She walked home with an extra bounce in her step.

"I'm going to miss seeing you two so regularly. But this is the last story. As soon as you approve it, I'll move into final edits and publication formatting." Gerry sat up straighter as she told Belle and Sally her news. "It's taken less time to finish the writing than I had thought."

"So do you have a revised estimate for a publication date? I'd like to get something in our newsletter and our website as soon release is imminent." Belle's business sense kicked in automatically while Sally was still adjusting to the idea that a book about Belle and her would soon be available to the general public.

"I think I can finish in about a month. It depends on how long it takes to get all the formatting done. It's very tedious. And it has to be done differently for the print version and the ebook version. Well, actually, for each kind of ebook device. Isn't that crazy that they can't agree on a common format?" She saw that neither of her audience understood what she meant. Oh, well, it didn't really matter. They didn't need to know. "Oh, but I do have some good news. I've lined up Ruth Welborne to trade off proofing."

"I didn't know she wrote," Sally replied, surprised.

Gerry chuckled. "Neither did she. In fact, she'd talked about hiring me to write her travel memoir. But she wrote a piece today about moving here that's really very good. I think she'll end up writing her stories herself."

"Oh, I'm sorry, Gerry. That leaves you without a job," Belle sympathized.

"It's really fine. I'll be okay financially with all the royalties we're going to make on **BellWhether Tails**. And I've got an idea for something else I want to write. I found out last night that Bradley King rescued Miss Velma Lee's journal from the renovation they're doing to her house. I'm going to borrow the book tomorrow from Betsy King – Bradley gave it to his mother – and see if I still get goosebumps."

"Why do you find that so exciting?" Sally inquired. "I think it's interesting, and I'd love to look at it, but it's not exciting enough to generate goosebumps."

"I'm not sure. I have an idea about using Miss Velma Lee and her sayings juxtaposed to my growing up down the street from her. I don't know how it will work, but I had a vision, I guess, when I heard about the journal. I could almost see my book laid out, chapter by chapter."

Belle's interest was piqued. "You writing a memoir?"

Gerry shook her head, "I don't know yet whether it will be fiction or non-fiction. I just know it weaves together my stories with Miss Velma Lee's."

"Well, I for one can't wait to read it," Sally declared.

"Would you read this first?" Gerry laughed, handing them copies of the latest chapter, the one about their moving to Plainview.

"Be happy to," Belle answered as Sally nodded.

"Then I'm going to leave and let you do it. Call when you're finished and I'll come get your edits." She left the two of them beginning to read.

"Thanks for calling Gerry, Mom," Hal told Betsy later that morning.

"No problem. I'm just surprised she's so interested in that old journal."

"I may be partially to blame for it," Hal admitted with a grin.

"How so?"

"Hang on a minute and I'll show you." Hal fetched his guitar. He tuned it before beginning the melancholy chords that introduced the melody. "I wrote this for you, but I played it for Gerry last night. I wanted another opinion." He sang softly, and Betsy listened with rapt concentration.

As the last chorus finished, Betsy brushed the tears from her face. "Honey, that is lovely. Thank you for writing it for me. Sounds like Gerry liked it, too." She sniffed and blotted a last stray tear.

"She did. She got really jazzed by the idea of reading Miss Velma Lee's journal. I think she wants to write about her somehow."

"So you two are seeing each other?" She asked cautiously. She was curious but didn't want to set him off again.

"Oh, I don't know, Mom. I'd like to. In fact, I thought about asking her to move to Colorado with me. But she won't go. She's settled in here. She's writing. It's the life she wants."

Betsy bit her tongue. She said nothing but merely nodded. She yearned to give advice, but she didn't. She was surprised that Hal had confided in her, and she didn't want to spoil the moment. She stood up to leave the room, patted him on the shoulder, and walked away. "I'm going to go read that journal," she called when she was safely away. She'd made it. She'd kept her opinions to herself.

Knocking on the door at Janie and Ruth's house, Gerry thought about the odd turns her plans had taken over the last twenty-four hours. She hoped Janie was home. She wanted to talk about what she was thinking.

Janie answered the door to a brilliant smile. "Wow, what a smile. Did I do something right?"

"Yep. You answered the door." Gerry gave her a hug. "I brought some proofreading for your aunt, but I'm dying for some chat with you. Do you have time?"

Janie glanced at her watch. "I have a couple hours before I have to do anything. So, yes. Come in. Want something to drink or eat?"

"Glass of water would be good." Gerry sat at the kitchen table while Janie filled her glass with ice. "Can we stay in here? There's something cozy about chatting around the kitchen table."

"Yeah, I know what you mean. Seems like nearly every good conversation I've ever had was at a kitchen table. So what's up?"

For the next two hours Janie and Gerry filled each other in on what was happening in their lives. Janie had Gerry doubled over in laughter when she described the building of the fort and its inaugural sleep-out. She also described the trip to Bristow's for Sesame Stix. "Hang on a minute," Janie called as she ran out of the room to her studio. She returned carrying several paintings that she laid on the table between them.

Gerry looked at them carefully, then chuckled, "You've co-opted Bristow's for your illustrations. That's wonderful! I love the homeless wee folk as clowns!"

"I like them, too. I haven't shown them to Chet, the author, or the editor yet, but I think they work. And I'd like them to stay in the book to help me remember the day."

"I doubt you'll forget."

Janie sniffed a laugh, "Me, too."

"So you're getting a little serious about Smoke, huh?"

"A little, I guess. He is one of the nicest people I've ever met. He's funny, and warm, and great with Jake and Oliver. And he's a wonderful gardener. Have you seen his woodland beds?"

"Don't forget, I grew up with him. He's still a testosterone-overdosed stinky adolescent in my book."

Janie giggled. "Oh, I knew so many of them in high school! But speaking of your book – how's it coming?"

"I've given the last chapter to Belle and Sally to read today. I'm done with the writing. But it will take me quite a while to get it formatted for publication."

"And then what?"

Gerry had been waiting for an invitation to tell Janie what was really on her mind.

"I don't think I told you that Hal and I were a hot item five years ago. I was crazy about him. Heard wedding bells when I was with him. And I thought he felt the same. Then one day he disappeared. Didn't call, didn't return my calls. After a few weeks of total silence, I heard from some of his friends that he'd moved to Colorado. And he told everyone that I broke up with him!

"I wandered around like the walking wounded for weeks. Then I slowly got over him. And now, when I've started to really get my life together, he shows up. It's not FAIR!" she yelled.

Janie said quietly, "Go ahead. Yell some more if you want."

"No, I'm done. I just wish I knew what to do about him. And you want to hear the real kicker? He wrote a song about Miss Velma Lee after Bradley found her journal – I'm dying to see that journal. I just know that I have to write about her."

Janie dropped her hand from her lip, "I think I just heard what you want to do about Hal. You want to write about Miss Velma Lee."

Gerry looked startled for a moment before nodding. "Dammit, you're right. But I did love him so!"

Janie nodded grimly, "I understand. Boy, do I. But sometimes we have to lay down our old treasures to have room to pick up new ones."

Gerry brushed away the few tears that had fallen, gathered up her things to leave, and mentioned the conversation she'd had with Ruth earlier.

"Ruth's serious about writing? I'll be damned," Janie responded.

"Not just writing. She's going to be my Proofing Pal."

Not to be outdone, Janie said, "But just you remember, I'm your praise-meister." Both laughed at their silliness. Gerry left the folders for Ruth and walked back to her house. She was exhausted from laughing and exhilarated from sharing.

Thirteen

"Only let strangers cut your hair; it's too personal for friends."

Velma Lee Lewis

At nine-thirty on the dot, Hal knocked on Gerry's door, Miss Velma Lee's journal in his hand. Gerry wanted to grab it from him, but managed to invite him in and serve him a cup of coffee before picking it up and holding it reverently.

"Do you think your mother will mind if I copy this? I think she'd like that better than if I kept it forever, which is my first inclination."

"I'm sure she won't mind. Where are you going to get it copied? I can take you there, if you'd like."

"What?" Gerry forced herself to close the book and pay attention to Hal. "Oh, I've got a scanner. I'll just use it. But thanks."

Hal saw her will her eyes to leave the book. He smiled sadly. It was cruel to keep her from reading it. "You know, Gerry, when I came home I had half an idea of inviting you to go back to Colorado with me." She began to say something, but he held up a hand. "No, let me finish. Of course, I wanted to see if we still had any of our old feelings for each other. I think the answer to that is an unqualified yes on my part."

"Mine, too," Gerry said softly.

"But I also saw something else. I saw how you've built yourself a life here. And that I can't ask you to move away from it. For one thing, I know what you'd say." He gave her a rueful smile as he reached for her. "Give me a goodbye hug. I'm going back to my life tomorrow."

Gerry wiped away a tear as she hugged Hal fiercely. "Take care of yourself. And stay in touch this time." She backed away from him and looked him in the eye. "I mean it."

He kissed her forehead, brushed his hand over her hair, and turned to go. He swallowed hard and said as he walked away, "Don't let yourself get sidetracked from becoming the writer you want to be. I know you can do it. I'm your biggest fan."

She watched him go with tears streaming. He was right, she knew. But. "It's those damned 'buts' that get you," she sobbed.

For several minutes, Gerry let herself grieve. Then the tug of the journal overcame the sadness. She poured herself more coffee, washed her face in the kitchen sink, and sat down with Miss Velma Lee.

She jotted down some of her favorite sayin's. One, she printed and taped to her mirror: "When you feel sad, cry and get it over with but not outside." She read the entire journal and reread some parts twice. Three hours had passed, and she was hungry.

Comfort food, she decided. Scrambled eggs or macaroni and cheese. Hunger won that battle – eggs were quicker to prepare. She got out the eggs and was reaching for the whisk when the phone rang.

"Hey, Gerry." Ruth said after Gerry's mumbled hello. "Did I wake you?"

"No, Ruth. I'm awake."

"I've finished proofing your stories and can bring them over if you've got time."

"Can you give me an hour? I'm just fixing lunch, and I need to take Jess for a run." Gerry hoped her red-splotched face would have faded back to normal by then. She wasn't ready to talk about Hal.

Ruth agreed and signed off. Gerry decided to work off her sadness. She was not going to allow herself to get sucked into the Miss Velma Lee material beyond scanning the journal before she finished *BellWhether Tails*. She'd just have to work like crazy to finish.

She'd start immediately. She'd do automated edits, build her templates and start formatting. She could add Ruth's edits to the mix as soon as she got them. And she could eat her eggs while she worked.

Ruth arrived just as Gerry and Jess returned from their walk. Ruth petted Jess while telling of the incomparable cuteness of Oliver. "I'm still expecting him to disappear. The way he came to us is hard to accept."

Gerry opened her eyes wide and hummed the theme from The Twilight Zone.

Ruth nodded. "Aliens or magicians, I figure."

"Or gypsies. Gypsies are always good," she opened the door to the house, waved Ruth in, and pointed to a seat at the dining room table where all her papers, books, notebooks, and laptop lay.

"I like your office," Ruth said looking around. "I mean, I really do. I'm not trying to be a smartass. I like it that you work in the middle of the house. I've never been able to do that. I get too distracted by everything around me. I need an isolation room."

"My house is pretty much an isolation room," Gerry noted with a shrug. "Here," she handed a small stack of papers to Ruth. "Your first blog entry with my edits and a few suggestions."

"OK, Proofing Pal. Here's your book marked up by me. I found a few typos – 'of' for 'on' and 'the' for 'she', but most of it was clean. I marked what I found in red."

"Any other suggestions or comments?" Gerry inquired as she looked through Ruth's markings.

"Well, really only one. I love the stories. You exactly caught Belle and Sally. And I think the structure – their alternating and describing important dogs – works well." She paused.

"I hear a 'but' coming. Oh, those damned 'buts'. I've bumped into 'buts' all day today."

Ruth took a breath, "You know my experience is in business writing. I'm not a literary critic." She paused a beat, "But. But I think the book doesn't end. It quits."

Gerry studied her for a moment then flipped through a stack of papers, stopped and read a page or two, then moaned, "Oh, dammit. I hate it that you're right. I'm not done writing after all!" She slumped against her chair.

"Is that a big problem?" Ruth asked gently, aware that she'd somehow caused Gerry more distress than she thought her suggestion warranted.

"No," Gerry sighed. "It's just that I've come up with an idea for my next project, and I'm eager to start it. But I need to finish the BellWhether piece first. And I'm not as nearly finished as I thought I was."

"Ah. Well, couldn't you continue formatting what you've finished while you think about what else you need? That shouldn't slow you down too much."

"You're right. I'll just keep going. Maybe I'll have a flash of insight in the middle of the night. If I haven't come up with an answer in a few days, could I borrow your kris?"

"It worked for Oliver." She patted Gerry's shoulder as she prepared to leave. "Don't worry. Keep working. I can find the door on my own."

Gerry called after her, "Thanks again, Ruth."

Standing in her renovated bathroom, examining herself in the mirror, Bea came to the sudden realization that she needed to renovate herself if she wanted people to accept her as Jo. She'd made a start. She'd begun wearing brighter colors. And slacks. And she'd gotten rid of the bun at the back of her head. But she wanted something more radical. Maybe she'd dye her hair maroon or get a tattoo. Or both.

She walked into her kitchen and smiled at how lovely it was. It took a fire to get her to change the kitchen. Maybe she needed to light a fire under herself.

Without giving herself time to change her mind, she sat down at her computer, searched for *New Beginnings Salon and Spa* in Enid, and called them for an appointment. With a mischievous grin, she made one for Sally, too.

Then she called Sally. "I've made you an appointment to go with me to Enid to a salon and spa. On Monday," she said flatly. "No argument."

"You've done what?" Sally asked with her voice rising higher than necessary.

"You heard me. You're going with me to Enid tomorrow afternoon. To the *New Beginnings Salon and Spa*."

"Well, uh, what if I have other plans?"

"Change 'em."

"Good Lord, Bea, er, Jo. You can't just bulldoze over me to get me to go with you." Sally was good at righteous indignation.

"Sure I can. That's what friends are for," Bea replied drily.

Sally sputtered a guffaw. "OK. You win. I'll go. But what about the diner?"

"I'm closing on Mondays. I need more time to myself."

"Well, Hallelujah! You should have told me that first. Then you wouldn't have had to strong-arm me." Sally was pleased that her friend was taking better care of herself. She'd nagged her about it for years.

"You know, Bea, Jo, Damn. I'm not good at coping with change. You'll probably always be Bea Jo to me."

"That's actually kind of cute. Bea Jo. I can deal with that."

"Or how about BJ?" Sally asked slyly.

"Don't press your luck."

"What time tomorrow?"

"We'll have to leave around noon. I'll pick you up. And Sal, don't tell anyone. Let's surprise them."

Leaving the salon the next afternoon, Sally caught a glimpse of their reflections in the shop window. If she hadn't known who they were, she would never have guessed.

Bea had dyed her hair – not burgundy – but a soft ash brown. Trimmed to chin-length, it waved softly around her face. And her face glowed from the facial treatment. She looked years younger.

Sally had cut her long braid off in favor of a short Judi Dench do that made her look like the Matron Queen of the Pixies. That itself was surprising, but the difference in her gait was what astonished her. The magic hands that had massaged her knee and leg had brought back more mobility than she'd had since she was shot. She thought it nothing short of a miracle.

Bea insisted that they each buy a new outfit to go with their new hair. Normally, Sally would have begged off. The walk-stop-wait choreography of shopping was horrible for her knee. But today it felt so much better, she was willing to try for a while.

Bea bought a pale blue tunic and darker blue slacks made of some light-weight floaty fabric. Sally's cotton-candy pink linen shirt over gray linen slacks heightened her new pixie look.

On the drive back to Plainview Bea chattered non-stop about her plans to change things in her life. "I'm going to change the schedule at the diner. I'll close Sunday and Monday, and every afternoon between one and five."

"That sounds perfectly reasonable, Bea Jo."

"Are you doing that on purpose?" Bea squinted her eyes at Sally.

"What?"

"Bea Jo."

"Sort of. Do you mind?"

"Not really," Bea admitted.

"New topic," Sally announced. "Is your sister coming tomorrow?"

"No. A week from tomorrow."

"OK."

"Second thoughts?" Bea asked with a frown.

"No. You?"

"Yes. I guess I'm feeling pretty ambivalent. On one hand, I don't know her and I'm not sure I want to. On the other hand, she's my sister."

"Yep. Blood complicates things."

"Do you think I'm making a mistake?"

Sally sighed. "I never had a sister. I don't know how that feels. But after all these years, Belle's like my sister. If she somehow betrayed me, I think I would forgive her. Eventually. And want her back in my life. Probably."

"That's what I think," Bea admitted. "I guess I'm feeling my age. I've cut myself off from all my family for years, and I think it's time to reconnect."

"Gather up your flock," Sally said thoughtfully.

"Huh?"

"Oh, it's something Belle said the other day. Ruth had asked her why anyone would want to tell a dog to come bye. You know, turn right and circle clockwise. Belle said you'd need that command if you were trying to gather up your flock. Like you are."

"I like that. I guess that is what I'm doing. And one little lost lamb will be here next week."

"So that's why the makeover? You want to look like Mary Contrary rather than Bo Peep?"

A couple hours later, Bea and Sally walked into the kennel office unannounced. Belle was working at her desk. She glanced up at them and asked, "Help you?" before she recognized them.

Her eyes widened, her jaw dropped, and she stared, unmoving.

Sally waved a hand in front of her face, "Hellooo! Anybody home?"

Belle slapped at Sally's hand. "Oh my God! I-I-I can't believe it! Look at you two. I can't believe it."

Bea asked Sally, "Is that a good 'Oh my God' or a bad one?"

Sally shrugged. "Earth to Belle. Earth to Belle."

"I am just gobsmacked. Never in my dreams did I expect to see Sally O'Neill without that braid. What made you do it, Sal?"

"I don't know. I saw how great Bea looked with her new cut and thought 'Why not? I can always grow it back.' So I did it."

"I think it was a good 'Oh my God!' after all," Bea's eyes sparkled.

Belle's head swiveled as she looked closely at each of them. "Ruth's right. There must be magic loose in the land."

Fourteen

"Never end something before you've begun it."
Velma Lee Lewis

In the following week, much happened in Plainview. Hal King went back to Colorado. Bradley King bought himself an old red Honda. Betsy King got Miss Velma Lee's journal back from Gerry Krane.

Everyone who saw them exclaimed over Sally's and Bea's makeovers. Ruth posted her first blog entry at www.hidden-in-plainview.com, her new website. And Win and Janie spent every evening together.

Win moved closer to Janie on the porch swing. "Are you chilly?" he asked as he pulled her into the circle of his arm around her shoulders.

"No. I'm fine. It's a nice night. I'm so glad the heat has finally broken." She enjoyed snuggling in the swing. It made her feel safe.

Win rubbed his cheek against the top of her head. "Janie?"

"Hmm?"

"Do you think we can go on the way we are?" he asked softly.

She straightened up and looked at his face. "What do you mean?"

"I mean, the more I know you, the more I want to know you. I'm not sure how long I'll be satisfied with just snuggling on the swing."

"Oh, I see. Well, what do you think the next step ought to be?"

He leaned down and kissed her. Gently at first. Then with more passion. He pulled back, slid her under his arm, and said slowly, "Maybe necking in the swing?"

Janie cocked her eye at him, crawled into his lap and kissed him soundly. As she wriggled away, she said huskily, "Oh, that can be arranged."

Win was faster than he looked. He lifted her back onto his lap and kissed her until her lips were bruised and his self-control stretched nearly to the breaking point. He disengaged her arms, stood up awkwardly, and announced, "I'd better go home while I still can."

Janie looked up at him from the swing. She saw a man she knew she could love. His pupils were dilated; his smile soft. She took his hand and led him into the house, closing and locking the door behind her. "I think you've waited too late already. You'll just have to stay here tonight."

The next morning as Win was getting dressed and watching Janie sleep, Jake burst into the room. "Momma, are you awake?" he yelled. He looked up and saw Win. He smiled in delight, "Mr. Mailman! Did you sleep with Momma last night?"

That woke Janie up. She sat up and pulled the sheet over her chest, "Jake, honey. Run downstairs and I'll be there in a minute to fix your breakfast."

"OK. Bye, Mr. Mailman!" Jake and Oliver tore down the stairs and into Ruth. "Guess what, Aunt Ruthie! Mr. Mailman slept with Momma last night." He ran on into the kitchen.

Ruth stood rooted to the spot, awaiting Janie's and Win's descent. As they walked past her, she said quietly, "I've only got one thing to say. Jake needs to call you something other than 'Mr. Mailman' if you're going to be here for breakfast."

Win exploded in laughter, soon joined by Janie.

"What's funny, Aunt Ruthie?" Jake insisted.

Win put his big hand on Jake's small arm. "Jake, I'd like for you to call me by my name. You can call me Win, like most everyone does. Or Winston, like my mother did. Or some of my old friends call me Smoke."

Jake scrunched up his face as he considered his choices. "I'm your friend. I'll call you 'Smokey!'"

"Smokey," Janie echoed as she patted Win's cheek. "You know what they say – where there's smoke, there's fire."

Win blushed ferociously.

Waiting together for the arrival of Ellen, Sally and Belle sat in the kennel office. Bea paced nervously from one end of the room to the other.

"Would you please sit down? You're making me crazy," Sally ordered none too gently.

"Want some iced tea?" Belle asked, holding up the pitcher.

"No thanks, it would just make me have to run to the bathroom even more frequently."

Sally shook her head, "I'm tea-ed out."

Belle, whose hearing was excellent despite her age, announced, "I hear a car." They all walked to the window to look.

Coming up the driveway was an old gold Cadillac. It sputtered and popped as it came. "Muffler," Belle declared. Bea and Sally looked at her in surprise. "What? I know what a worn out muffler sounds like."

The Cadillac pulled into a parking space, and Ellen Murphy got out of the car. Bea went out to welcome her with a hug.

"I'm sorry I'm late but the directions said to turn at the large oak tree and I did but it must not have been the largest tree since I got lost and had to turn around and luckily met a guy on a tractor who directed me here," Ellen told Bea in a non-stop stream.

"Oh, Lord," Sally muttered.

"Shh," Belle cautioned.

"Belle and Sally, I'd like you to meet my sister, Ellen Murphy. Ellen, this is Belle Sheppard and Sally O'Neill."

"It's nice to meet you, Ellen," Sally said graciously, offering her hand.

Ellen stood immobile for several seconds before extending her hand and giving Sally's a firm grasp.

Belle shook Ellen's hand also as she said, "I hope you had a pleasant drive."

Ellen sucked in air in preparation for a verbal outpouring but Bea interrupted her. "Shall we show Ellen around the place before we go inside?"

Belle took the lead, walking Ellen through the kennel buildings, the training center, the barn, the apartment on offer, and finally the office and their home.

Ellen said little during the tour. When they got inside, she looked crestfallen.

"What's wrong, Ellen?" Bea asked.

"I can't see anything here I could do. I don't know much about dogs, although I like dogs. I'm not like some people who are afraid of them or anything."

Belle responded, "We need people to do things other than work with the dogs. We need someone to help in the office – answering the phone if we're not there, working with the training schedule, handling registrations of the dogs, booking travel for people coming to classes or to pick up their dogs."

Sally added, "We also could use help in our house – housekeeping, laundry, some cooking. Or if you're interested in learning about the dogs, you could work with the puppies and eventually help train them."

Bea looked at her sister's wide-eyed stare. "Ellen, does any of that sound attractive?"

Ellen shook herself, "I'm not great with paperwork. But I can clean house and cook. And I'd like to learn to work with the dogs."

It was Bea's turn to look surprised. Ellen had answered succinctly and clearly.

Sally took Bea's arm, "Let's let Belle and Ellen discuss the particulars while we go fix some snacks."

Belle began, "I know you're nervous. But it's okay. Sally and I don't bite." Ellen nodded uncertainly. "Here's what I propose. We will hire you to work forty hours a week. You will spend twenty-five hours working at our house doing housekeeping and cooking some meals. The other fifteen will be spent socializing puppies. I suggest you begin your day with the puppies and finish at the house so you can cook our dinner several days a week."

Ellen nodded, "I can do that."

"We'll pay you six dollars an hour and let you live in the apartment rent-free. You'll want to clean it up and paint it, I imagine, before you move in. We'll buy the paint if you do the work."

Ellen nodded again. "That's fine. I can do that."

"So when could you start?"

Ellen thought for a moment, "Beginning of the month?"

Belle replied, "That will be fine." She put out her hand, "Deal?"

Ellen shook it, "Deal." Then she covered Belle's hand with her other hand and whispered, "Thank you. I get so nervous around Jo. I run off at the mouth. I was afraid I'd blow it with you, too."

"Shh. You did fine," Belle assured her. "And give Jo a chance. She's a good person. You'll like her."

"Oh, that's not the problem," Ellen said. "It's the other way around. I'm afraid she won't like me."

"She'll like you. Just relax," Belle patted Ellen's shoulder as Sally and Bea reentered the room with a tray of snacks and drinks.

"We've got it all worked out," Belle told the others. "Ellen will start working here at the beginning of the month." She picked up a glass of tea and saluted Ellen. "Here's to the newest member of the BellWhether Family."

Rising blood stained Ellen's cheeks. "I haven't had any family for years, and now I have two." She smiled at Bea.

Bea took Ellen's arm, "Let's go to my place and let you get unpacked. Then we'll go to my diner for supper. Would you two like to join us?"

Sally and Belled exchanged a look. "Yes," Sally answered. "That would be nice. We'll meet you there at six."

Bea led Ellen to her house. "Here let me help you carry in your bags," she said when they arrived.

Ellen shook her head. "I only brought this," she held up a small case.

"OK. Then come on in and meet Shep, my roommate." She opened the door and Shep dashed out. He wove between the two sisters, sniffing Ellen as he did.

Bea started into the house, but Ellen turned back to her car. She'd forgotten her purse. On a whim, Bea threw out her left arm, made a circling motion toward her chest, and told Shep, "Come bye."

He ran to Bea's right and circled Ellen. As she walked to her car, Shep came in closer, nudging the backs of her legs with his nose.

"What's he doing?" Ellen asked, a little frightened of this strange behavior.

"He's herding you. Gathering up the flock. He doesn't want you to wander off or get lost. Or be alone. He wants the flock together," Bea smiled at Ellen. "And so do I."

Stacks of papers littered the table in front of Gerry, Sally, and Belle. Gerry was describing the choices she had in mind for fonts, margins, gutters, and headers. Sally struggled to pay attention. She could see that Belle had already given up the fight. Her blank expression hid wherever her mind had wandered.

The phone rang. Both Sally and Belle grabbed for it. Belle won. She answered it normally, listened, sucked in her breath, and said, "Yes?" She stood and walked out of the room, listening to the person on the other end of the line with rapt attention.

Gerry barely paused. She asked Sally if she had a preference for page numbers at the top of the page or the bottom.

"Gerry, honey, I don't know a thing about book production. But I trust you. Put it together, and let us see it. I'm sure we'll agree with you. Are you totally finished with it except for the formatting?

"Not really. I'm stuck. Ruth and I both think the book needs another chapter, something to bring it to the present, but I don't know what. I've got notes from stories you two have told me about some of your other BellWhether champions, but none of them has what I'm looking for."

"What are you looking for? Maybe I can help."

Gerry took a deep breath and slowly released it. "That's just it. I don't know what I'm looking for. Just something to give the book closure."

Belle walked back into the room carrying the phone. "Who was that?" Sally asked.

Belle's face glowed as she answered, "Mary Nell. She's coming to the Herding Instinct Test on Saturday with the puppy – she named it Heart. And she's bringing Bitsy, her granddaughter.

"She said they'd stay overnight at the Edith Motel and have time to visit with us on Sunday, too. She's eager for Bitsy to see our kennels. Said she's a real dog lover."

"That's wonderful, Belle." Sally smiled delightedly. Then she turned and looked at Gerry's folders and papers. "Gerry, would you excuse us for a moment. I need to ask Belle something. Could you go to the kitchen and get us all some more iced tea?"

Gerry nodded, puzzled, but went into the kitchen as asked.

"Belle, Gerry just said she needs another chapter to give the book closure. You know the perfect story."

Belle looked at Sally carefully. "OK. But you tell it."

"Are you sure? Don't you want to tell it?"

"Can I have veto power?"

"Of course," Sally said softly.

"Then you tell it. Do it now. Before I change my mind." She left the room for the screened-in porch, pulling the door closed behind her.

"Gerry, can you come back now?" Sally yelled.

Gerry came in carrying three glasses of tea. "Where's Belle?"

"She had to leave. But we agreed that I would tell you a story. We think it will be the perfect ending for the book." She left the table and walked into the living room, to a leather-covered recliner next to a reading lamp. "Get your pad and pencil. Come in here and get comfortable."

Gerry complied, curling up on the sofa, with her pad and pen at hand. Sally leaned back, closed her eyes, and began, "I'm going to tell you the story of BellWhether's Unforgotten Treasure."

BellWhether Tails

BellWhether's Unforgotten Treasure – 2011

One of the hardest things about loving dogs is the shortness of their lives. Thorpe, Miss Kitty, Dillon, Nosy, Dusty, Skye – all gone to their well-deserved rewards. Our cemetery expanded every year.

I had just had to put down another old friend and was feeling melancholy, reminiscing about my many great dog friends when Belle came bursting into the office.

"I think I'm finally going to get pups out of Magpie. I just palpated her and felt at least three walnuts."

"Birth follows death follows birth," I said.

She looked at me with raised brows, "You okay?"

I nodded and tried to switch gears. "When are the pups due?"

"Five or six weeks, I think." Belle had become a good substitute vet, able to handle many of the routine medical tasks for our dogs. It is a necessity when you live so far from a veterinarian.

We'd lived in Plainview for about twenty-five years. We'd built up the BellWhether Kennels name, whelped, trained, and trialed many champions.

And we'd built a good life. I'd gotten past my resentment of my disability. Whenever I got to feeling too sorry for myself, I'd remember Belle telling me in exasperation not to bury my heart in my wounded knee. That always made me smile.

Belle had gradually lost her fear of Benton. Even after she learned of his death, twenty years ago, he continued to haunt her, but she'd gotten tougher over the years. She kept the fear in a little box and only opened it on rare occasions.

I glanced fondly at her as she sat at her tidy desk sorting though her mail. I shuffled through the top layer of papers in front of me. Where had I put that letter from the Kansas Bureau of Investigation inquiring about man-

trailers? I'd sat back and closed my eyes attempting to visualize where I'd put that envelope when I heard Belle gasp.

I whipped around to look at her and felt a stab of fear. All the color had drained from her face. A hand was on her chest, and she took shallow, ragged breaths. "Belle? Belle, are you okay?" I tried to remember everything I knew about first aid as I stood to go to her.

She looked up at me then, and I saw astonishment rather than pain in her eyes. "What is it?" I asked quietly.

She shook her head, unable to speak, and pushed a piece of paper at me.

I hobbled to her without my cane, took the page, and nearly fell as I tried to read while hopping back to my desk. I flopped into my chair, read through the letter quickly, then read it again.

Dear Belle Sheppard,

On March 23, 1939, in Memphis, Tennessee, Julia Edith Campbell was born to Charlotte Jane Campbell. Father unknown.

The baby girl was put up for adoption immediately by the mother who was using the stage name, Lola Bell. The baby was adopted by Leon and Edna Smith. Leon died of alcohol complications in 1954. Edna Smith lived until 1980.

In 1957, a detective hired by Bess Campbell of Kansas City, located Edie Smith, originally Julia Edith Campbell, in Southaven, Mississippi, living with her 2-year-old daughter. Two weeks after being contacted by Miss Campbell, Edie abandoned her daughter to the care of Bess Campbell.

I am that daughter.

Are you Julia Edith Campbell?

Sincerely,
Mary Nell Campbell Floyd
Floyd Farm
Blue Fork, Arkansas 72633
mnf@floydconstruction.com 479-555-1234

"I'll be damned! Your daughter! She found you through your Aunt Bess," I said at last. The color had returned to Belle's face, and her breathing sounded normal. "What'll you do?"

She squeezed her lips into a grim line and shook her head quickly from side to side. "I – uh – I don't know. I've always been afraid this day would come. And always been afraid it wouldn't."

I read the letter again. "It's a very unemotional letter."

"Yeah, I don't know what to make of that." Belle ran her hand through the hair hanging on her forehead and swept it back with a practiced motion. "Let me see it again."

I hunted for my cane. I didn't want to chance another hop across the floor. But Belle came to me this time. I handed her the letter after rubbing and patting her forearm. "It'll be okay." She nodded uncertainly as she left the kennel office for our living quarters. I knew I'd find her on the screened porch sitting in her big wooden rocker, rocking and worrying.

For over a month after Mary Nell's letter arrived, I watched Belle worry and stew but kept my mouth shut. Finally, I could contain myself no longer. I burst in on Belle while she sat in the living room reading. "Dammit, Belle. You owe her a response."

She went rigid.

I had a piece of BellWhether Kennels letterhead and a black ballpoint with me. I thrust them at her. "Write to her this minute!" I had seldom demanded that Belle do anything even though she falsely accused me of being bossy. But this time I was adamant, and she knew it.

She took the pen and paper from me, slammed the paper onto the table beside her, and wrote, "YES" in heavy lines. She shoved the paper back toward me. "Satisfied?"

I took the paper, nodded curtly, and stomped off to the kennel office. I shuffled through several stacks of papers until I found the copy of Mary Nell's letter that I'd secretly made. I'd read it many times, convincing myself that Mary Nell sounded unemotional out of fear not anger.

Before I changed my mind, I picked up a pen, drew a line under Belle's terse response, and wrote a conciliatory note: "Give her some time." I signed it, folded it, put it in the envelope, addressed it, stamped it, and drove into Edith to mail it.

After dropping the letter in the mailbox, I wished for about the millionth time that I could buy a beer in this town. I settled for a cup of coffee at the Edith Diner.

Bea was her smiling self. I returned her cheery greeting with a mumbled, "Hey."

"Something wrong, Sally?" she asked as she poured my cup of coffee.

"You don't have anything to put in this coffee, do you?"

Bea's eyes widened.

"Never mind. I'm just a mess."

"Wanna talk about it?"

"Yes, but I can't. I got in the middle of Belle's business, and I shouldn't have. I think she's really pissed."

Bea looked me over. "Let me feed you. You'll feel better, and Belle will have time to cool off."

"OK, but not much. My stomach's in my throat."

"Drink your coffee and calm down. I'll be right back." Bea hummed something cheerful as she bustled to the kitchen. In a very short time she delivered a stack of pancakes, two strips of bacon, and two over-easy eggs. "Comfort food," she said as she refilled my cup.

I sat there for two hours, eating and laughing at Bea's stories of the lost tourists who had been there yesterday.

With my good humor and courage restored, I left Bea a big tip to compensate for her refusal to charge me for the meal. I drove home and found Belle in her rocker. I sat on the porch swing opposite her and said as contritely as I could, "I'm sorry, Belle. I should have stayed out of it. It's not my business."

She rested her mouth on her fist and looked at me over the top of her glasses. "Did you mail it?"

I nodded, "Yes."

"Well, it's done then." She leaned her head back against the rocker, took a deep breath, and began to rock furiously.

I watched her for a few minutes before going inside. She'd come around eventually, I hoped.

That night Magpie went into labor. Even though she was five years old, this was Magpie's first litter. It took her about eight hours to deliver five puppies – three girls and two boys; one blue merle girl and the rest black and white. A pretty litter.

Belle forgot about being angry with me as we moved into our familiar roles of midwife and puppy nurse.

One afternoon about five weeks later, I was sitting at my desk planning my next training class. I thought I might be able to train five new handlers rather than my normal four if I got some help. Bradley King, who helped out around the kennel when he was out of school, would be ideal. He was smart, willing, and great with dogs. I'd have to schedule my class to match his break. As I reached for the phone to call his mother to check on his schedule, a tap on the door announced a visitor.

I looked up from my schedule and did a double-take. A younger version of Belle looked uncertainly at me. "Help you?" I asked.

"I'm Mary Nell Floyd. I'm looking for Sally O'Neill."

"My God! I guess you are! You look so much like her it takes my breath." I stuck out a hand, "I'm Sally O'Neill." She shook my hand with a firm but damp palm.

"I saw her out in the pasture. She looks like my grandmother."

"Likely. You look like she did fifteen or twenty years ago."

"I'd like to talk to you. Is there somewhere we can meet? I know she's not ready for me, and I'm not sure I'm ready for her, but I want to know about her. Will you?" She was trying to be business-like, but the crack in her voice as she asked if I'd meet her revealed the extent of her nervousness.

I agreed to meet her for dinner at the Edith Diner. She left, heaving a deep sigh as she stepped out the door. I watched her drive away, then went to find Belle.

"Hey," I yelled to her as she trudged up the drive from the training paddock. "Meet me on the front porch when you're finished." She waved at me and followed a young dog into the first of our four kennel buildings. I couldn't tell which dog it was. The sun was in my eyes, but I still found it worrisome. Then a smile came to my face as I heard my Gran's voice tell me, "Stop troublin' over trifles."

I made a pitcher of lemonade and carried it to the porch. I sat down to wait for Belle, rehearsing how I'd tell her about our visitor.

When she arrived, she made it easy for me. "Who was that tall gray-haired woman who was here a little while ago? She looked familiar."

I stalled as I poured her a glass of lemonade and carried it to her. After I sat back down on the porch swing, I answered, "That's what I wanted to talk to you about. That was Mary Nell."

Luckily I'd seen her go pale before with no ill effects or I'd have been dialing 9-1-1. "Take a deep breath and have a sip of lemonade," I advised.

"She came," Belle whispered as she steadied her shaking hand.

"She said she didn't think you were ready to meet each other yet, but she wanted to know about you. I'm going to meet her for dinner in Edith."

The stunned look hadn't left Belle's face yet, but she nodded comprehension, "What will you say?"

"I'll answer her questions as honestly as I can. Are you okay with that?"

Ice clinked in her glass as her hand shook raising it to her mouth. She took a long drink, then looked me in the eye. "I trust you to do the right thing."

Now my hands shook as I realized the responsibility I'd taken on. "Dear God, don't let me screw it up," I whispered as I reached for my own glass. "Want a splash of gin in that lemonade?" I asked as I headed for the liquor cabinet inside.

"Whatever," Belle said, her mind far away from lemonade on the front porch.

I opened the liquor cabinet but instead of gin, I pulled out two bottles of Merlot. I'd take them to dinner. "In vino veritas," I said in a ghastly Latin accent.

Getting through dinner with Mary Nell was easier than I'd imagined. I liked her. She was wryly funny, self-deprecating, and open about her feelings. I answered her questions about Belle and asked some of my own. A glass of wine over dinner helped steady both of us so that when we went to her room at the motel to continue our conversation, we were fairly relaxed.

The hardest part was answering Mary Nell's question about why Belle had never looked for her. I'd had trouble with that myself. But I told Mary Nell what I'd come to believe: Belle had been far too frightened of Benton when he was alive. Afterwards, she thought it was too late. It would take time for Mary Nell to digest that. Hard truths don't go down easy.

I stretched the truth a little and told Mary Nell that Belle was *eager* to meet her. Maybe *eager* and *terrified* aren't too far apart. At any rate, she left me that night with a promise to come to see us the following morning.

Then I had to tell Belle.

As I expected, she was waiting for me on the porch. I told her about our dinner and filled her in on the biography of Mary Nell: she was married, happily, to Walter Floyd; she had two sons, Dub and Jif; Dub had been married and had a child, a five-year-old daughter named Bitsy.

"I'm a great-grandmother. Oh my God! I was hardly even a mother, and I'm a great-grandmother." It was the only time I'd ever seen Belle totally dissolve into tears. "I missed too much," she said when she got herself under her usual unyielding self-control."

"One more thing, Belle. She's coming to meet you in the morning at nine o'clock. I told her you wanted to see her."

She nodded in resignation. "Then I'd better get some sleep." She started to go inside but turned back to me. "Thank you, Sally," she said softly before disappearing through the door.

Belle was up, dressed, and sitting rigidly on the couch when I stumbled out of my room the next morning. I don't know how long she'd been up, but from the dark circles under her eyes, I could guess she'd gotten little sleep.

"Want some toast?" I asked on my way to the kitchen. It was eight-thirty. I'd intentionally stayed in bed until the last minute. I was nearly as nervous as Belle.

"No. It's too late to eat," she snapped.

"OK," I sang out. I wasn't going to let her use anger at me to distract her from her fear. I'd seen her do that before, usually to my detriment.

I fixed toast and coffee and pretended to read a book while surreptitiously keeping one eye on the slow-moving hands of the clock.

Just as the big hand hit the twelve, I heard the door in the kennel office open with a jingle. I hurried down the hall and found an ill-looking Mary Nell hesitating in the doorway.

"Come on," I told her, "it'll be all right. She's as afraid as you are." I gestured down the hallway. "Come on. I'll be there."

Mary Nell followed me down the hall and into the living room. Belle stood as we entered, then walked toward Mary Nell and extended her hand. "I'm Belle Sheppard. Welcome."

Mary Nell introduced herself, shook Belle's hand, and stood in the middle of the room shell-shocked. I steered her to a chair and left the room on the pretence of making a pot of tea. I was too tense to watch.

About fifteen minutes later, Belle found me in the kitchen. "You can come out now. She's gone."

"I was just...um..."

"I know. It's okay." She sat down across the table from me. "God, I'm glad that's over." She picked up the empty teapot and set it back down. "I'm glad it happened, though. There's never been a day since I sent her to Aunt Bess that I haven't thought about her. Worried about her." She played with my teacup, spinning it in its saucer. "She's turned out fine, though. Just fine." A small smile crossed her lips. "We'll see what happens next."

I put my hand on top of hers and gave it a slight squeeze.

She smiled at me. "She liked the puppies."

"Damn. I forgot to tell you. She used to herd with a border collie."

Belle nodded and swiped at a stray tear that tracked down her cheek. "Thank you, God," she whispered.

For the next couple of weeks Belle alternated manic activity with rocking on the porch. She spent hours with Magpie's puppies, evaluating their conformation and temperament. She dug through old files, looking for something. She didn't say what.

Then one morning at breakfast, she announced that she was going to drive to Oklahoma City that day to ship a puppy.

"Oh. I didn't know you'd sold a puppy. Which one?" I asked.

"The blue merle bitch."

I looked up in surprise. "I thought you were going to keep her. Didn't you register her?"

"Yes. I named her BellWhether's Unforgotten Treasure. I need to remember to tape this envelope onto the crate."

I picked up the envelope as she rummaged through a drawer looking for tape. Inside the envelope were three items. The registration form for the puppy, an invitation to a Herding Instinct Test, and a yellowed piece of stationery with a gaudy letterhead.

Belle watched but said nothing as I read the hand-written page dated 1960. I recognized Belle's writing and her story. She wrote it her first night in Dodge City where she'd run to escape Johnny Benton.

I thought I knew what she was doing, but I flipped back to the registration form. Yes, she'd transferred ownership to Mary Nell Floyd.

"When did you decide to do this?" I asked gently.

"When I decided that my great-granddaughter needs a puppy."

About the Author

Kathy Wagenknecht lives behind the nursery she operates just outside Little Rock, Arkansas, with her three border collies, two Cardigan corgis, and a talented painter. Visit her at her website: kathywagenknecht.com.